"Is it all right if I kiss you?" Brace asked.

"Please." Destiny turned her head, catching his mouth, loving the gentle strength. Her heart slammed into her chest at the well-remembered passion built rapidly. "Brace . . ."

"Ummm?"

"Nothing. Doesn't it seem unbelievable?"

"No. I've dreamed of this many times."

"Umm. Maybe that's why you're good at it." He smiled against her mouth. "Bet on it."

"A hundred bucks says you're not better, but the same."

"Easy money for me."

"Oh? We'll see." She wrapped her arms around his neck.

Their bodies fit as though they'd never been apart, sliding down on the silky sheets, pressing together, needing to find the wonder.

His hand slipped up her side, curving under her breast, closing over the fullness.

His breath sighing into her mouth had the hotness raging through her.

"I love you and I don't give a damn if it doesn't fit the ground rules," he muttered.

WHAT ARE *LOVESWEPT* ROMANCES?

They are stories of true romance and touching emotion. We believe those two very important ingredients are constants in our highly sensual and very believable stories in the LOVE-SWEPT line. Our goal is to give you, the reader, stories of consistently high quality that may sometimes make you laugh, sometimes make you cry, but are always fresh and creative and contain many delightful surprises within their pages.

Most romance fans read an enormous number of books. Those they truly love, they keep. Others may be traded with friends and soon forgotten. We hope that each LOVESWEPT romance will be a treasure—a "keeper." We will always try to publish

LOVE STORIES YOU'LL NEVER FORGET
BY AUTHORS YOU'LL ALWAYS REMEMBER

The Editors

DESTINY
SMITH

HELEN
MITTERMEYER

BANTAM BOOKS
NEW YORK · TORONTO · LONDON · SYDNEY · AUCKLAND

DESTINY SMITH

A Bantam Book / May 1998

ISBN 0-553-44629-0

Published simultaneously in the United States and Canada

Bantam Books are published by Bantam Books, a division of Bantam Dou-
bleday Dell Publishing Group, Inc. Its trademark, consisting of the words
"Bantam Books" and the portrayal of a rooster, is Registered in U.S.
Patent and Trademark Office and in other countries. Marca Registrada.
Bantam Books, 1540 Broadway, New York, New York 10036.

PRINTED IN THE UNITED STATES OF AMERICA

OPM   10 9 8 7 6 5 4 3 2 1

ONE

It was pure self-indulgence! No doubt about it, Destiny Smith thought as the plane circled to land.

Hawaii had been a logical choice. The corporation, of which she'd become the major stockholder at the death of her father, would now be under her control. She needed to consider where she'd have her base of operations. The corporation owned a fine beach house on Maui, but she wouldn't necessarily be alone there. Her relatives felt free to come and go there as they pleased. So she'd booked a hotel room in Waikiki instead. She'd relax there and list her alternatives as chief executive officer of Smith-O'Malley.

Not in a million years had she ever considered running her father's corporation. She had thought he would be around forever. She had loved her chosen work, the job she had studied and trained for. She'd been a capable agent for the FBI.

After settling in at the hotel, she wandered outside, driven by her turbulent thoughts. She paused along the beach, the hot sun beating down on her. Kicking at the sand, she sought strenuous exercise, desperate to drive some of the demons away.

Not too far from where she stood, a surfing class was being formed. Frustration catapulted her toward the circle of people. Nothing else could have driven her to the water sport after years of avoiding it like the plague. She'd never been a jock, not as an undergrad at Stanford or in graduate school at UCLA. She had, of course, gone through the rigorous training the FBI insisted on, but as a rule, she avoided sports.

What would her relatives think if they could see her now? she thought as she chose a surfboard. No doubt they were paddling about in the warm ocean that fronted the airy beach house on Maui. Like many of the corporate assets, it had belonged to Destiny's mother and father, and now was part of the estate belonging to her.

After instruction, then practice with a veteran surfer, the class was encouraged to go out alone. Destiny did, time after time. She seemed to be getting better, staying on the board longer. She paddled out to deeper water.

She'd always thought surfing was insane, similar to sailing out the door of an airplane. But despite developing cramps in her arms and shoulders from the everlasting paddling, she was enjoying the challenge of trying to stand on a wooden board that was shaped like a shark and just as nasty. Keeping her head down, she churned with her arms, determined to get up and stay up, even if she ended in traction.

"I don't think you heard Bernie."

"Huh?" She looked up at the stranger who had one hand on her board.

"Your class is that way."

The water had slicked his hair to ebony. His eyes would have seemed the same jet color if not for a sapphire glint. His richly distinct voice penetrated the roar of the ocean and her concentration, making her turn on her board and look the way he was pointing. "Oh. Pardon . . ." Her board flipped and she went with it, swallowing some of the Pacific as she kicked up. She pushed at the arm around her. "Thanks." *Cough, cough.* "I'm all right. I know how to swim. Excuse me, I have to get my board."

"I have it. You shouldn't be this far west. The waves are geared to more experienced surfers."

"Gotcha. Thanks for the direction. I'm all set. I'll be able to find my class." She grabbed her board, swinging her other arm to include her group. They weren't there!

"You're about a mile beyond them," the man said. "I told Bernie I'd tow you back."

"No need. I can— Good Lord! Look at that wave. I'm trying for that one."

"Wait! Listen—"

Concentrating on the monster at her back, the roar of it blurring his words, Destiny aimed every decisive bone in her body at riding the wave. Clambering up on the board, she glanced over her shoulder, eying the aqua giant coming at her. In her peripheral vision she noted the man next to her readying himself. Heavens! The wave was the size of her office building, and it sounded like rush hour. No matter. This time she'd get on, and get up.

She felt the first push and popped to her knees, holding the board as she should. Then, as though a hand from the deep lifted her, she stood, turning her left foot, then her right until she looked at the beach, but her feet faced parallel to it.

Power struck behind her, lifting her and the board. At the sudden hefty surge she wobbled, slipped, then steadied into a crouch, awed at the force. She felt jerked into the air by powerful wings. She teetered, bent back and forth, but stayed on and didn't tip. The ride lasted only seconds, she was sure, but it felt like a wild and woolly hour-long trip into another world. As the wave died and swept away, she lowered herself again to her board, out of breath and laughing.

Exhilarated, she had a moment's pause when she noted just how far she was from the beach, and even farther west than she'd assumed after speaking to the stranger. Oh well! She began to paddle toward the east.

"Wait!" the man called. "You'll have to stay on now. Get ready. Don't look back. Here comes another one. Take your position on the board. Good girl. Stay focused."

Was he an instructor too? she wondered.

Bronzed though he was, he didn't look as Hawaiian as Bernie. Still, she listened and obeyed.

She rode high in the air, the water screaming and creaming out behind her. Never had she felt such a sensation. Bizarre! Charged! Wonderful! Lifting, lifting! She thought she was going to be thrown up to the clouds.

Was it seconds, minutes, or hours that she rode that billowing, bellowing mountain of water? For long moments she wavered, not sure if it would take her down and under in a roll that had caused more than one surfer serious injury. It seemed even stronger than the previous wave. It was curling more, her board trembling in response. The water wasn't flattening out as it had before. Instead it corkscrewed under itself. For a time she thought she was going out and down with it. Then, like a dream, she rode the curl for just a moment before she was past it. She was out of breath, exhilarated, still in a crouch and still on the board! Lordy! It was fabulous!

The water didn't exactly flatten out even after the wave had passed, but it was smoother. She sank down on the board, elated, delighted, speechless. When the man came up next to her, she couldn't stop grinning. When his frown turned to a smile, she laughed out loud.

"You took a big chance coming over this far," he told her, maneuvering next to her board.

"Not really. What I mean is, I didn't know how far over I was. I was thinking about something else."

He shook his head, smiling. "Can't do that when you surf."

"I guess not." She exhaled. "I tried it several times before, but didn't make it to my feet. That was my umpteenth try." She grinned. "And I got up."

"I know, but this is not where the learners belong. Experts surf here, and sometimes even they get into trouble."

She looked around her. "I *am* too far from my class, aren't I?"

"Yes. I can steer you back if you want to grab my ankle." He angled closer. "You handled your board well."

"Thanks."

"I'm Brace Coolidge."

"I'm Destiny Smith. Sorry, I can't reach that far. Assume I shook your hand."

"Done."

When he laughed, her heart flipped over, then rose up and choked her. "I don't have time for men."

When he laughed harder, she realized she'd spoken aloud. Maybe her blush would look like sunburn. She was bound to get one, even with sunscreen on, sitting out on the board as she was, legs, arms, and face exposed. Even if the sun god didn't burn her, the sea god facing her would set her on fire with flaming ocean water. He was one sexy guy.

"How about one more time on the board and we'll discuss it," he said.

"Sorry. What I said was gauche. A case of a mouth out of control."

"You're an up-front lady. Not a bad thing. Let's try again. This time we'll go a little closer to your class."

"Okay." So she'd die from sunburn. Better than getting struck by an eighteen-wheeler . . . or not seeing the sea god again. What had he called himself? Racehorse?

Until they got into what he termed safer water, she did hang on to his ankle. Damn, it was a thrill!

"I can manage now," she said, though she didn't want to let go of him.

"Good."

Paddling her board next to his, she tried for a sangfroid attitude and turned to melting butter instead. He should get a permit for that look, she thought. It was more lethal than an Uzi!

Positioning their boards on the beautiful water, they looked behind them. The waves here were slower and lower.

"You'll be bored," she said to him.

"No I won't."

That sexy grin! She swallowed a mouthful of seawater and coughed.

He moved closer and patted her on the back.

She closed her eyes, feeling caressed. Lordy, he was potent. She needed to think of something else.

She glanced in front of her. Her hotel looked so small from her position out on the water. It was like being on a desert island . . . with a sea god. The idea had appeal. She felt good, more calm than she had in a long time.

"Heads up, Destiny! Here's a good one."

She looked over her shoulder and grinned, readying herself. When she felt the thrust, she went to her knees. Once more she stood, not nearly as steady as the man near her, but not falling either.

They rode the waves again and again. She was limp with exhaustion and—as bizarre as it seemed—passion by the time he called it quits. How could you fall in love when you were being pummeled by the Pacific? It was crazy.

"You need to get out of the sun," he said, "or you won't be able to move tomorrow."

She grimaced. "I guess you're right." Actually her thoughts weren't on her skin, they were on his, and the rest of his body. What great eyes, deep green with a golden aureole, not blue, as she'd thought at first. His lips were firm, beautifully shaped and sexy. His hair could be dark brown, but in the sun it was auburn fire. Better not to look lower in the clear water, she told herself, or she'd start salivating.

How had he dredged up such feelings? She'd been too wrung out by the job since her parents' deaths nearly a year earlier to involve herself with anyone. Most days she had milk and a sandwich for dinner, retired early, then rose with the sun to battle through another mountain of problems at Smith-O'Malley.

One day there'd be a love interest, no doubt someone she'd known forever, whose family was familiar to her. She'd pictured an easygoing relationship, with mutual respect and a commonality of tastes and interests.

That had flown out the window on a surfboard. Nothing would be so smooth and well planned with . . . whatever his name was. In an hour or so, he'd made oatmeal of her dispassionate view of a future with a man. He had her reeling, limp as a dishrag. The emotions seething inside her had nothing to do with good planning. It was down and dirty lust and need.

When they returned to the beach, Destiny went with him while he stored his board. Then she had to return hers and endure Bernie's lecture on paying attention, and how she'd endangered herself. "I'm sorry."

"You should be. Next time by the rules. Okay?"

Destiny nodded. As they walked down the beach she eyed her grinning companion. Pausing, arms akimbo, she raised her chin. "Don't be so smug. One day I'll be better than you on a board."

"I don't doubt it."

His smile broadened, and her heart flipped in her chest like a sea trout in a pan. Hyperventilating, she hardly noticed the itch behind her knees that told her the sunscreen had failed.

She held out her hand. "Thank you for the lesson in surfing, Brace." She'd finally gotten it right after hearing Bernie call him by name.

He shook her hand. "I'll walk with you."

He went with her into the hotel and up the elevator. "I'll wait here," he told her, lounging against the wall outside her room.

She took a quick shower, then smoothed on a medicated cream. The whole time, her mind was on the man in the hallway.

After donning a flowered muumuu and sandals, she went to the door and opened it a crack. He was still there! "Hi."

"Hi. I'd like to invite you to my place for the afternoon."

"You would?"

"Yes."

"All right." She locked her door and accompanied him to the elevator. Life had taken a turn when she met Brace, she realized. She'd never be the same. "Should we walk?" She couldn't clear the huskiness from her voice.

"I have a car."

"Oh."

The lobby was packed with people going in and out of the doorless hotel, and they passed numerous other people as they walked the two blocks to his car.

Destiny found it strange that no one noticed her glow. Maybe Hawaiians walked on air themselves, so they didn't notice when she did. Nice people. Looking up at the sky, she studied the cerulean surface. She couldn't see the planets, though she was positive her aura would be noticed on Mars. No one else caught on, though. People could be so unobservant.

The traffic in Waikiki was horrendous, but Brace didn't seem to mind it. Stop and go. Honking horns.

Screeching brakes. Throngs on both sides of the street. Then all at once they were on a winding road and there was only the muted roar of the Pacific and the purr of the car. "Is this your own road?" she asked.

"It belongs to the Bird of Paradise Hotel. I have a place there."

"Oh."

When he said nothing else, she scanned his profile. "I don't usually go to people's homes when I don't know them. Not a good plan."

"I don't usually invite people I don't know well."

"Oh." She studied the thick greenery that lined the road, then looked back at him. "What're you thinking?"

He didn't answer as he steered around a curve and parked in a huge area, shaded and flowered, looking more like a park than a parking area. He switched off the ignition and turned to her, his left hand on the steering wheel, his right hand on the back of her seat. "You're a funny, beautiful, gutsy lady. Even with the water splashing between us, the waves rushing at us, I knew you had brought . . ."

"What?" she asked. Puzzled, she stared at him. His smile crooked in a sexy way and he caught a tendril of her hair.

"I thought you'd brought such grace to my life," he said, his voice so very quiet.

"You did?"

"Yes." He touched her hair. "I love these red-gold curls that sweep your shoulders. Your eyes have the aqua cast of the ocean. Maybe you're a sea goddess."

"That's what I thought about you," she blurted, then grimaced.

He grinned. "Thank you."

"Thank you," she whispered back, feeling fuzzy and outrageous.

"You're welcome." He slid out from behind the wheel and walked around to the passenger side.

He reached in to help her from the car, then kept her hand in his as they walked to a door. No lobby, she noticed, just a single opening into an elegant one-story building. A suite belonging to the exclusive Bird of Paradise.

"It's lovely. I'm impressed."

"I was hoping I could impress you."

Surprised, she looked at him. "Why?"

"You've knocked me out, lady. Everything else has faded since meeting you, Destiny Smith." His matter-of-fact words, the slight smile, the quirk of one eyebrow emphasized his words.

"Let me change," he said. "Promise you'll be here when I come back."

Destiny nodded. In minutes Brace returned to her in sandals and a silk flowered shirt that was tucked into loose trousers of a similar silky fabric.

In silent consent they strolled along the beach. Then they returned to the suite.

After mai-tais, the fruity rum concoction that could pack a punch like a boxer, dinner was served to them by white-coated attendants, silent and efficient.

The lei placed around her neck had a gingery scent. She had no idea what she ate, except it was light, aromatic, and excellent.

When the dishes were cleared away, Brace took her hand and led her to the terrace. The sun was dipping low. "It's going to be a beautiful evening," he said.

"Uh-uh." Destiny was afraid to talk. She and Brace seemed to be in such a bubble of sweetness. Gentle breezes touched her skin with pleasing coolness. It seemed like only minutes passed before the sky became so cluttered with stars, Destiny fancied there was gridlock up there. The moon was so silvery orange, it looked freshly painted.

"Wonderful, isn't it?" Brace said against her ear.

She nodded again, loving the feel of his mouth in her hair.

"Let's walk."

Like two children, they carried their sandals and held hands, walking along the beach in the other direction.

"I wanted to show you this cove. The water's perfect. Let's swim."

She blinked up at him. She had panties on under the muumuu, nothing more. "I'm—I'm not sure that's a good idea."

"I'll agree it could be more than swimming. You've pulled me like iron to a magnet from the first time you looked at me."

She thought of many excuses she could give him.

Instinct told her he wouldn't press her. He stood a foot from her, but didn't try to kiss or coerce.

Drawing in a deep breath, she looked into his eyes. "Let's get naked. I don't want to get my dress wet."

Laughing, he stripped off his own clothes. "Last one in buys the mai-tais."

Yelping at the challenge, she threw down her muumuu and sprinted for the water, hitting it in a flat dive that carried her out. "I win," she shouted.

"Cheater." He splashed her and she sprayed water back at him.

When they ran out of the water, laughing and dripping, he threw his shirt at her. "Dry with this." Then he stared at her. "You're more beautiful than a Hawaiian evening, Destiny."

She patted at her face and body with his shirt, her hands shaking, not embarrassed though he continued to stare at her.

"Look at me," he said.

She tossed his shirt to him. "Dry yourself."

Grinning, he caught the shirt and slapped at his body. "I'd like to kiss you."

"Sounds like a plan," she said, her voice rusty and rich.

He stepped closer, then paused, looking at her and shaking his head. "Unbelievable. I never thought to find you." Taking her face in both hands, he leaned forward and pressed his mouth to hers. Kissing her deeply, he let his tongue caress hers, catching her gasp in his mouth.

All the lost moments of all her yesterdays, her fears, her determination, her pain, each and every bit of caring she'd ever known, was in the kiss she received and gave back to him. It spilled from her lips into his mouth as she stood on tiptoe to take all of him she could. Beautiful Hawaii lost its luster, giving it to Brace. Everything faded away but him as he became the largest and brightest star in the firmament, his tall, muscular body hard and thrusting as he moved closer. She wanted him. No! She needed him. Simply that.

Moments later—years later—he released her, studying her, tracing her features with one finger, then lowering his hand to circle her breasts, touch her middle. "That wasn't a casual kiss. You know I want you. You can feel it, see it."

She nodded, again readying excuses. Instead, the truth came out in a gush of air. "I'm vulnerable, Brace. That's not something a person's supposed to admit. But I have to tell you something else that's pathetically corny. I'm just not into one-night stands."

Before he could respond, she held up her hand. "Neither do I want a commitment from you or anyone. I need to do some healing for myself. I'm a mess, mostly from the job I have. It's wrung me out. I'm in Hawaii to repair." She shrugged. "From all I can tell, that's best done alone."

He stepped back.

She moved forward. "You have to know something else. You might be the Band-Aid I need . . .

and I'd want that, but there can't be any more. Too much in my life needs sorting."

"As I said, you're an up-front woman." Irony backed his smile. "So? What's the deal? Go directly to jail, do not pass Go? A passion-filled moment of time . . . or do we hold hands while I grit my teeth?"

Laughter burst from her at the ease with which he took her ultimata. "I'm a fool. I'll admit that."

"I won't argue."

Humor had no place in such a passionate moment, but she couldn't contain her laugh. "The hell with it. I'll heal in another time and place. Let's have great sex." When his jaw dropped, she giggled.

"Do you suppose," he asked, "we might tell jokes *after* we make love? Or is this a New Age development?"

"I—I think we should try it without the laughter," she said, and dissolved into mirth again. "Oh Lord, this is awful. No one acts like this." Gusts of laughter shook her as the foolishness of the moment rolled over her in waves. They were naked. He was gorgeous. She wanted him and couldn't stop laughing.

"This definitely will be one for the books," he muttered against her hair as he caught her in his arms.

"We could videotape it and send it to Guinness," she said, looping her arms around his neck, still feeling light and giddy, but heavily laced with passion.

"Let's practice first," he said against her mouth.

"O-okay." When his tongue skidded across her cheek and entered her ear, her knees gave way. "You're bringing a good bit of power to this project."

"And meeting some potency along the way."

"You think I'm potent?" Batting her eyes at him, she had to wonder when she'd felt so good. She couldn't recall. Maybe never.

"I do."

"Great. I've always wanted to step up to the plate."

"Cliché, but cute."

"I like being cute."

"Get all your ducks in a row," he muttered, his mouth scoring her neck.

"Another cliché," she told him.

"I've got more," he breathed into her ear.

"Right," she murmured, her eyes closing. There, right at that moment, on a beach in Hawaii, she was holding a man she'd known mere hours as though she'd never let him go. She wanted him with a hunger she'd never felt before, sliding her hands over his body, loving the indentations, the body hair, the muscles and sinew, everything about him.

She'd never pictured herself going ballistic over a man. Certainly she wasn't a ho-hum, you've-seen-one-man-you've-seen-'em-all type of gal. But this was brand new, a never experienced sensation. Could she ever have foreseen the volcanic emotion she was feeling with Brace Coolidge? He had a silly name, but she loved it. She thought the man embracing her the most beautiful human, with parts so exotic they made her mouth water. She was wild to have him.

"You're so wonderful, Destiny Smith. I've never known anyone so lovely."

That might have stopped her cold, overused line that it was, if she hadn't been so damned heated. He was making things up to get her into bed. So what? She was gangly, too tall, with more angles than curves. "Nope," she said. "Too boney."

His chuckle set off a fire on her abdomen. "No way, sweetheart. You've been put together by a great artist, and I love every pore."

She misunderstood him. No one used the "L" word unless they were totally out of the loop. He probably meant lust. She could understand that. Could this wild, swirly feeling last, or would it pop like bubble gum? Who cared? She had it now. If this was all there could be, she could hug it and hide it in her memories.

He took a deep breath. "Let's go back to the suite."

They ran along the sand and into his place. In the bedroom they fell across the bed.

He lifted her into his arms, taking her breast into his mouth and suckling there. All thought vanished. As if a steel door had clanged shut, her focus left the outside world and centered on the man who held her. Every nerve in her body, every cell, fixed on the man holding her. She heard someone call out his name, but her body was writhing so much, trying to get closer to him, she didn't recognize it as her own voice.

As his mouth moved down her body it was as though he were setting her on fire. Too out of breath to tell him she wanted more, she was tearfully grateful that he must have heard her mind cry to him. He answered with hands and mouth.

When his tongue lapped her hips, moved lower to center on her womanhood, entered there, she shouted. Stunned, surprised, totally thrown off stride by the surge of passion, the raw want, the blistering need that had her grasping him, she could only hang on and pray he wouldn't release her.

The thrusts of his tongue took her beyond imagining into a whirlwind of fire that swept her into an explosion she'd never experienced or even imagined.

"Shh, darling, you're not through yet." Moving up her body, he entered her gently, beginning a new rhythm at once.

Destiny tried to form words. They wouldn't come. She wanted to tell him she understood his plan and approved. Taking her with him into infinity was perfect. When she thrust against him in blatant demand, he didn't hold back.

Wave upon wave of wild emotion took them deeper into a sea unknown by most, needed by all.

In one cataclysmic joining, they were tied to each other forever with one incredible, unforgettable orgasm.

Stunned, she lay beneath him, coming back to the world slowly. "Never . . . never thought it could be like that," she muttered, not even sure she'd spoken out loud.

Brace kissed her hair. "Neither did I." He chuckled, though there was a tremor in his voice. "You are so wonderful."

"You get high marks too," she said, her eyes still closed, smiling when he laughed. "I don't know what to say."

"And we were only practicing."

Laughter caught her and she clung to him. "I think you're supposed to have a cigarette, not laugh," she instructed.

"All right. Next time we'll put more into it."

She chuckled. "Too late. I think we went over the top this time."

"Well, we'll polish it up before we call Guinness."

"You're terrible."

"Not me." He kissed her. "I might agree it should be in the record books."

"You're a nut. I like that."

"And I like you." He kissed her. In moments they were on fire again.

"Honestly," Destiny said when she caught her breath, "this has to be unusual."

He grinned. "You make me laugh, beautiful. I love that."

They made love again and still couldn't release each other. When they looked into each other's eyes, there was no looking away.

"Do you find this as astonishing as I do?"

Destiny asked, her mouth against his. "I mean, it's not just because I haven't done much rehearsing, is it?"

"I'd say you're well beyond expert."

"Great. It's nice to be good at something."

"Be proud of yourself, because you are." He shook his head, then fastened his lips to hers again before speaking. "I swear to you, I never imagined anything like this in my life. I mean that."

"Good."

Exhausted, replete, they fell asleep in each other's arms.

Before dawn he woke her. They made love again, quick and hot. Then they embraced and were soon asleep once more.

When they woke later, Brace treated her sunburn, they made love, ate breakfast, and swam. They didn't part even to shower.

Her sunburn faded by the third day. Once she thought of calling her family, then forgot it. No time. She and Brace had spent two of the days in bed, though they'd talked of surfing again.

"Marry me, Destiny," he whispered to her naked body.

"Yes," she whispered back.

They were married by a judge, and left for Tahiti that afternoon. A passionate and deliriously happy honeymoon followed. She called her family from there, ecstatic, sure she'd found the key to everlasting joy with her wonderful husband.

TWO

Five years later—Yokapa County, New York

Divorce!

A word rarely mentioned in her rigidly conservative family. Destiny had not spoken to her relatives since she'd signed the papers. Not that they'd ever liked Brace, but they found the ending of marriage, in and out of the courts, repugnant.

Destiny didn't need the everlasting repetition of I-told-you-so lectures. They were more than a pounding head could take. Nor did she want to hear their observations on looking before you leap, or sticking to your own kind. Since she'd generally eschewed most clichés, she'd opted out. Going to ground was the only viable choice.

A friend, Divinity Brown Blessing, had offered the sanctuary of the New York countryside. She'd taken it, renting one of the condominiums owned by

Divinity and her husband, Jake. She simply couldn't deal with her family. It was no balm to her spirit that the mutual distaste between her family and Brace had made some of the arguments on both sides irrelevant. Early in her marriage she'd made it clear she wanted to hear nothing derogatory about her husband. Most of the time her wishes were honored, but their feelings about Brace hadn't changed.

Looking out the window of the condominium, she stared at the sparkling blue lake that fronted the property. "Mom and Dad, what would you have said about this mess? I need you."

A cardinal, whistling in the trees, was the only answer. "Maybe you're right, bird. I'll blow them all off for a time." Her parents would have liked Brace, would have admired his business acumen that was much like theirs.

She recalled her phone conversation with her uncle the night before; he had pontificated—as usual—about her life and the business. She'd finally cut him off. "I'm sorry, Uncle Tyrrell," she'd said. "I've made my decision. I'll handle the corporation from here. Ryan Porter will take care of the day-by-day details at the head office in San Francisco."

"Stay there and rest if you must," Uncle Tyrrell had said. "I can handle the company—"

"No. I'll be in touch with the office every day. That's the way it's going to be."

Destiny ambled out onto the deck. Inhaling deeply, she pressed fingers to her temples. Getting better had to be her priority. Her friend Divinity agreed.

July heat bounced off Cayuga Lake, rippling the surface. Perfect for swimming, she thought. After changing into a bikini and a terry cloth jacket, she slipped a towel, snorkel and mask, and earplugs into a canvas bag, then dropped in her keys. Donning beach shoes, she left her bedroom through a door that led to the deck. She paused to look at the view again. Blue sky and emerald water. Cream and silver waves. Beautiful.

A flight of wooden steps led down to a narrow front lawn. Across the sloping greensward was a cliff. The steps leading from there to the beach were wide and solid, made of cypress. A boogie board leaned against the railing, anchored there by marine hawser. More than once she'd wanted to test her mettle on the freshwater waves. She couldn't chance it, though. Quite sure her mind would instantly crowd with memories of that day she'd met Brace off Waikiki Beach, she avoided the anguish.

Leaving her bag on the landing about six feet above the beach, she descended, then strolled across the narrow, gravelly strand.

Slipping into the silky fresh water, she donned the mask and sank down, swimming easily in the clean, green depths. Swimming alone had its dangers, but she found it salubrious to the spirit. She never went beyond a neck-high depth, keeping it manageable in case of trouble. Maybe it wasn't smart, but she needed the lake's soothing.

Minutes passed without registering. It surprised her when she lifted the mask and eyed her diving watch. She'd been in an hour. Common sense told her it was time to get out. She was a distance from her condominium. Actually, she was closer to where Divinity and Jake lived.

She looked up at the Blessing house to see if either was on the terrace. No one.

Thinking of her friend made her smile as she left the water and started walking back to her own strand. Engrossed as she was, the voices didn't register at first. When they did, she was so surprised, she stopped and listened. Children on her beach. She smiled. Loving children was second nature to her.

She rounded a shallow bend and frowned. They were the dirtiest pair she'd ever seen, and they were scrounging in the plastic rubbish cans left at intervals along the shale-strewn edge.

"Hi."

At her voice, they spun around like tops. The smaller of the two, a girl, wailed, then stuck a soiled thumb in her mouth.

"We ain't doin' nothin'," the boy said.

"We aren't doing anything," Destiny corrected, hoping her emphasis on what was said, rather than their deeds, would distract the frightened duo. It might even keep them from running.

The little girl's eyes bugged. "*We* aren't either."

The boy glared at her, then at Destiny. "I know what you were doing. Changing the way we speak."

"Correcting your usage," she said in the same

careful tone. "Join me for breakfast? Cornflakes and strawberries, and lots of orange juice?" Their swallows were almost audible. "C'mon. I hate to eat alone."

The boy lifted his chin. "I ain't . . . aren't . . . am not scared of you."

"Good. I'm not scared of you, either. My name's Destiny. What's yours?"

"Don't tell her," the boy said through his teeth.

"Ella, but Clyde calls me Stinky."

"Oh? I'll call you Ella."

"Okay."

"How about you?"

"Clyde calls me Jerk."

"His real name's Jeremy," the girl offered.

"I like it. Let's go." She led the way up the stairs, holding her breath. When she bent to pick up her bag, she looked under her arm. They were following! She said nothing as she mounted the rest of the stairs and crossed the lawn to the condominium. She could hear them muttering behind her.

She walked around to the main entrance, rather than enter her bedroom, and got out her keys. She'd just begun an amiable monologue about the hawks and eagles that liked to dive-bomb her deck when another voice joined hers.

"You could always charm a crowd."

The voice seared and speared. Every drop of her blood fell to her ankles, then dribbled away. Choked, she spun toward him. "Brace!" He was propped against a stanchion supporting the overhang, looking at her through the screening that formed a shallow, protected porch.

"Go away," Ella said. "We're to have st'awberries."

Jeremy shushed her.

Brace straightened, pushing open the screen door and walking toward them. "Nothing to say, Destiny?"

"Go away," she whispered, her throat raw.

"See!" the little girl said, moving closer to Destiny, who put a hand on her shoulder. "Who is he?"

"My ex—"

"Her husband. I haven't signed the papers, love."

"Don't call me that."

"Introduce me to your friends."

Destiny turned her back on him. "We're hungry. Sorry. See you another time." She was so frazzled, she couldn't speak to him with any modicum of calm or good manners. What were the children's names? Better yet, what was her ex-husband doing there?

A native Californian descended from a line starting with the conquistadors, he had similar coloring. His dark brown hair was straight and thick, with a gray streak above his left eyebrow that had started a couple of years earlier. An older woman at Smith-O'Malley had called him a modern-day Rudolph Valentino, the heartthrob of the 1920s. When Destiny had looked at a copy of *The Sheik*, she had agreed, to a point. The silent-screen star resembled Brace, except her husband was taller, with far more presence.

His eyes were a dark green with a gold aureole; his cheekbones were wide, suggesting his Viking ancestors on his father's side. His face looked hewn from granite until he smiled. Then his sensual lips curved over white teeth, emphasizing the dimple in one cheek and the cleft in his chin. He was too sexy by far. He should have been a movie star, instead of the owner of a studio that hired them. That was just one of the many businesses in his family conglomerate.

His well-toned body enhanced the silk suits he usually wore, day and evening. Now, however, he was dressed in jeans. At least she thought that's what he was wearing. She was having trouble with her key. Damn thing wouldn't go in the lock.

"How are things in the rarified atmosphere of the Mendez-Coolidge Corporation?" she asked through her teeth.

"Fine."

"Ah, yes. So fatiguing checking on offshore drilling, publishing, and let's not forget wine and film making." The key slipped into the slot and turned. One minor triumph despite hands slick with sweat. Only Brace could make her steam like a radiator.

"I manage."

She turned blindly to the children, barely seeing their features through the haze of uncertainty brought on by Brace. "Come along. We'll get our strawberries."

Even through her own uncertainty she could see their wariness. Her tongue untied itself with a vengeance as she looked down at her grimy guests.

"He's a well-known wine maker, but we only drink New York wines here. Mendez-Coolidge chardonnays and merlots are only two of the many types of wines they have, and they're competing nicely with their French counterparts. But . . . we're doing the same in this section of New York. How about that?" As she chattered on, she was fuzzily aware of the children's blank stares as she ushered them into the condo. "Old Californio money, don't you know, from the Mendez family. It mixed nicely with the gobs of gold belonging to the Coolidges."

"Destiny," Brace said, his voice low. "They don't understand your underlying waspishness—"

"Waspishness? Ridiculous. I haven't even warmed up to our own little business arrangement—"

"Destiny!"

"Aren't we getting strawberries?" the little girl asked, worry tinging her tone.

"Of course we are. You'll see them on the kitchen counter. All washed and ready to eat. Now, what was I saying? Ah, yes. We were discussing our merger, or as some called it, our marriage—"

"We weren't," Brace interjected.

"Smith-O'Malley combined with Mendez-Coolidge." She spread her arms, knowing she was acting like a fool, unable to stop. "We became a conglomerate, while other poor slobs were just wife and husband. Whoopee." She hesitated, tried to smile at the gaping children, fumbled with the keys in her hand, then slammed them down on the library table in the foyer.

She couldn't tell Ella and Jeremy how passionate they'd been with each other. They couldn't be informed how she and Brace had lighted the nights, glorified the days with their torrid joinings. They'd disagreed on many major points, including how she spent her time, how he spent his, their families, their social activities, but they'd been in full, hot agreement in bed.

"Time to eat now?" Ella asked in a small voice.

Ashamed, Destiny nodded. "Right away."

"I'm hungry for strawberries too," Brace said, catching the door she would have closed behind the children. "How gracious of you to invite me."

She turned toward him when she reached the kitchen that was separated from the spacious great room by a breakfast bar. "I—I might not have enough."

"It'll stretch."

His smile didn't hide the hardness in his tone, the flinty expression in his eyes.

She lifted her chin. "I guess it'll have to do." Her jaw unclenched when she noted how the children watched her, the boy eying the door. "Would you two like to see how the hot tub works?"

The little girl grinned, but when she moved forward, her brother held her back.

"What?"

"You're going to cook us," the boy blurted out.

His sister's eyes got round, the thumb retreating into the mouth.

Brace frowned, his lips forming a protest even as Destiny's raised hand silenced him.

"No. I'm not. I like children. Let me show you." She turned and walked across the kitchen to a small room that had a tinted glass wall overlooking the lake. The hot tub was in the center. She turned on the bubbler, then slid the glass doors back to let the sunshine stream in.

As the water bubbled and frothed, she climbed up the short ladder and down into the tub. "See?"

"We'll get our clothes wet," Jeremy said.

Since their clothes didn't look as though they would last in any water, Destiny thought fast. "Right. Let me call a friend. In the meantime—"

"I have to use the bathroom," Ella said.

"Right." Clambering out, Destiny felt as though she was caught in quicksand, not a hot tub.

Brace studied her as she climbed out of the tub, showed Ella the bathroom, and pointed out another one to the boy. She was thinner, but still beautiful. His gaze followed her when she went to the phone not far from either bathroom. He didn't overhear her conversation, though he noted she smiled once, even laughed. After hanging up the phone, she convinced the two children to get into the tub in their underpants, which were more gray than white and torn in several places. Then she scurried to the kitchen, keeping one eye on the hot tub while she got out bowls, cups, and glasses.

"See?" she called. "I'm right here. You can watch me set out the food. Isn't the hot tub fun?"

The two heads nodded, the smiles tentative. When the boy cuffed some water at his sister and she returned the shot, they began to play in earnest.

Brace concentrated on the children and their awestruck remarks about the hot tub, not totally sure they wouldn't drown. Their experience with water seemed limited. After a few minutes, seeing them play and splash each other was too tempting. He'd left his ditty bag on the front screened porch, though.

"You guys," he said to the children, "no rough-housing for a few minutes. I'll be right back." It made him uncomfortable when they went motion-less, staring at him. Who the hell had made them so fearful?

He fetched his bag, ducked into one of the bath-rooms, and was back in no time, dressed in swim trunks. He climbed into the tub, ignoring their wide-eyed stares. Reaching behind him, he grabbed a small rubber ball and skimmed it across the surface to the boy. "Tell me your name."

"Jeremy. My sister's Ella."

"Hi. I'm Brace."

"Is that a name or a nickname?" Ella asked.

"Both, I guess. I was named John Braceland Coolidge the Third. Since my dad was called John, my grandfather Jack, they called me Braceland. Then it became Brace."

"Oh," they said at the same time.

Brace sensed that not many people answered their questions.

Destiny came through from the kitchen, carrying a tray with three glasses of orange juice, her head down as she balanced the drinks. "Sorry. I didn't mean to be so long. I hope you were careful. I called a friend. She's sending . . ." Her voice trailed off when she looked up right into Brace's eyes. "You're in the hot tub." The breathy words held a question . . . and an answer.

"Yep. Join us, or would you like us to come out to drink? I assume one of the juices is for me." He knew by the blinking of her eyes it wasn't, that Destiny was frazzled and was fighting her way back to calm. "We'll be out in a minute."

"Ah, right. Drink the juice. I'll get the cornflakes started."

"They don't take long to cook." He saw her back stiffen. When the children chuckled, she turned around, her expression softening.

"No, they don't," she said, smiling at the two youngsters. "My, you look just fine. Do you like it?"

The little girl laughed and nodded. The boy was slow to show his approval. It came in a short up-and-down jerk of the head.

Destiny risked the fragile connection. "Where do you live?" The question stopped their breathing, brought the children back to the brink of panic.

She cleared her throat, regretting pushing that button. Too soon. "Let me start again. My name is Destiny Smith—"

"Coolidge," Brace added, his expression bland when she sent a narrowed look his way. "I know you didn't use my name that much, but we aren't divorced. The papers aren't signed, as I said."

Taken aback, she stared at him. "Then . . . then do it."

He shook his head, and turned to the children. "And my name is . . . ?"

"Brace," Jeremy said.

"Right. Good boy. But remember, don't be impressed by names. Only people count."

For some reason, Brace's remark upset the children. Destiny saw Ella's eyes puddle up, and Jeremy looked anxiously toward the door again.

"Whatever is frightening you is no more." Brace's flat statement turned three heads toward him. "From now on you're under my protection."

"And mine," Destiny added.

"That means no one's going to hurt you."

"You don't know Clyde," Jeremy said.

Brace inclined his head as though pondering the remark. "I don't think I do. Is he big?"

"And mean. And he don't"—Jeremy glanced at Destiny—"doesn't mind breaking your fingers. Said so." The boy's head jerked up and down for emphasis. "He hurts."

"Does he?"

Destiny held her breath. Most people didn't

know when Brace was in a fury. He always hid it behind that satiny tone. She coughed, gathering their attention. "I . . . we don't care about his size. Bullies will be handled. Would you like to stay here for a while?"

Brace sat up straighter. She knew he was trying to catch her eye.

"Can we?" Ella asked.

"Yes, but I do have to talk to someone who will want to talk to you about Clyde. Is that all right?"

"Don't tell Clyde," Jeremy said.

"I have no intention of speaking to him," Destiny said in her loftiest tone.

"That tears it," Brace muttered, slumping back down in the hot tub.

The doorbell chimed, making the children stiffen.

"Clyde," the little girl muttered.

"Nonsense," Destiny said, grinning. "I'm sure it's my friend."

Brace jumped up in the tub. "Let me answer it."

"Certainly not, you'll get the floor all wet. I'll be right back."

Just to make sure, she glanced through the peephole in the front door before opening it. She recognized the workman from Jake Blessing's construction site. She opened the door.

"Darnell, isn't it?"

The man nodded. "Yes, ma'am, it is. Jake wondered if you were all set on food and things. I brought some, along with the clothes you need." He grinned. "Jake has sources for everything." He handed her the almost full shopping bag, along with another smaller, lighter one topped with clothing and footgear. "Jake said I was to check things. I didn't recognize that car out back. We don't have much call for a Jaguar. Is it yours?"

"A friend's."

"There was a guy on the power pole up the ways. I don't know him. Know most of the linemen in the area. If you don't mind, I'll tell Jake about that."

"Thank you. I'd appreciate that."

"Glad to help, Miz Destiny."

"Thank Jake and Divinity for me."

"I will, ma'am." He tipped his cap and closed the door.

She walked back to the hot tub, her fingers itching to get the children into the shower and shampoo their heads. Don't push it, she told herself. Another time.

"Here's some old clothes a friend sent over," she said to the children. "They thought I might've damaged yours. Try them on, if you please."

When they got out of the hot tub and dried, she gave a small bundle of socks, sneakers, jeans, T-shirt, and underwear to Ella, and a similar pile to Jeremy. Each headed toward the bathrooms they'd used for undressing. She turned toward the hall leading to the kitchen.

"Nothing for me?"

"Not a thing." If only her voice hadn't quavered. His laughter followed her like a silk whip, arching her spine. She breathed a sigh of relief when he went into the second bedroom to change. She scurried into her own bedroom and shut the door, locking it.

Hands shaking, she undressed, cursing under her breath. She took a slapdash shower and dried herself as though Satan were on her tail. Wasn't he?

Dressed, she stared into the full-length mirror on the back of the bathroom door. "You are in control of your life. No one else." She shook her finger at her reflection, then opened the door. She took several deep breaths before leaving the bedroom at a trot.

The children were sitting at the kitchen table; Brace was leaning against the breakfast bar.

Destiny ignored him and went to the cupboard, bringing down three different bran cereals. She set the strawberries next to them, then found cantaloupe and milk in the fridge.

Brace unbent himself from the counter to get silverware and dishes. It was almost like the early days of their marriage, when they hated being apart and were so hot for each other they couldn't pass without kissing. He caught her gaze. She could feel the blood run up her neck. Damn him! He knew she was remembering.

THREE

"Destiny, this could be touchy." Divinity Blessing eyed her friend, tapping the papers on her desk. Tall, auburn haired, slender with only a slight tummy bulge to say she was pregnant, she was every inch the able attorney.

"I know," Destiny said.

Divinity cleared her throat. "Let's deal with the issues at hand. First, I called Sherwood Dinsmore, an attorney in Jake's father's old firm. I filled him in on everything. He's good and very happy to help." Divinity's smile was wry. "Jake's furious. He feels he should have known about the abuse."

"Oh, I think Clyde sounds cagey enough to protect his investment. Probably the children were rarely seen."

Divinity nodded. "No doubt he was living off a stipend meant for the children. Jake will have the whole county on his ass." Divinity riffled through the papers. "I also called a friend who specializes in the laws pertaining to child custody and abuse. He says we could be walking on eggs, but there might be precedents for what you want to do. If there's a loophole, he'll find it . . ." She looked up when there was a knock at the half-open door. "Come in." Brace entered the library of the The Arbor, Divinity's home. "Hi. I was just telling Destiny about some legal advice I've gotten."

Brace nodded. "Jake just told me about it. It matches up with what my attorney said. Jake gave me your friend's name and number. I'll pass them on to my attorney so they can talk."

"Good." Divinity looked at Destiny, obviously puzzled. "You two seem—"

"Nothing's changed," Destiny said.

"I see," Divinity murmured, though her expression said she didn't see at all.

Destiny rose and went to her friend, kissing her cheek. "Have to go."

"I'll work on straightening this out. From what the kids have told you, and I'm sure it's sketchy, they've had a tough time." Divinity grinned. "You love them already, don't you?"

"I do." Destiny felt Brace's hard stare, but didn't look his way. It was enough he'd managed to lease the condo next to hers. He'd been there six days, and she was still as shaken as she'd been on first seeing him at her place. Though she'd told him flat out she wouldn't let him stay under her roof, every night she tossed and turned before she slept, wishing him by her side, wanting him to embrace her. Damn him! Thank goodness for Jeremy and Ella. They intrigued and delighted her in so many ways. They'd also occupied so much of her time, she barely had a moment to worry about Brace. The children and the corporation were all she could handle. Even if he never left her thoughts, she was determined not to fret about him.

"I've moved next door to Destiny," Brace said abruptly to Divinity, "so I'm keeping a watch on the place."

"Wow!" Divinity looked from Brace to Destiny. At Destiny's glower, she swallowed her grin.

"Take care of yourself, friend. I'll be back," Destiny said, whirling so fast she almost stumbled. She went past Brace at a gallop.

"I'll expect you," Divinity called after her. Then she glanced at Brace, inclining her head. He shrugged and looked after Destiny. "Nothing personal, Brace . . . but if you hurt her again, I will personally knee you in the balls."

He laughed, shaking his head. "Why are tough women my weakness?"

"A touch of class?"

"Ouch. I'm fighting for my world, lady. Cut me some slack."

"Maybe I would if I didn't know how fragile Destiny is right now. She's been wounded and I don't like it." Divinity bit her lip. "She could use some loving care."

"So could I," he snapped, then rubbed his hand down his face. "Sorry. I'm working on it."

Divinity almost smiled. "I'd wish you good luck, if it weren't for past circumstances."

"Things aren't always what they seem."

"I'm not the one who needs convincing. She is. I admit you'll still have to drastically change my opinion."

"I'll try my damnedest." He sprinted from the room, Divinity's low laughter following him.

Out in the hallway, he looked down the mahogany-lined staircase to where his wife seemed caught in a conversation with the houseman, who was handing her a pile of children's clothes.

"But I'm going shopping," she protested, "and—"

"These will do you until then," the houseman pronounced, then turned and walked toward the back of the house.

Destiny looked up and saw him on the landing. Instantly she headed for the door. Just as quickly he started down the T-shaped staircase.

"You can run, but you can't hide," he said, reaching the foyer just as her hand touched the doorknob.

Her back stiffened, though she didn't turn. "I wasn't running."

"Sure you were, but we'll forget that. I didn't know we were adopting."

" 'We' aren't. Besides, it's still in the planning stage."

"Look, my love—"

"Save it," she said through her teeth.

"All right. We'll do it by the book. Destiny, you're still my wife under the laws of California and the country. I haven't signed the papers."

"I'll fly to the Dominican Republic and—"

"Don't bother. I'll sign them . . ."

Her heart fell to her shoes.

". . . after a suitable grace period." He held up his hand when she spun around and would've retorted. "Since the children will be mine under the law as well as yours, I suggest a compromise. We work together on this, get the legal work done to protect the children, then discuss our problems. It doesn't seem right not to put them first. Doesn't it make sense to build a fence around Ella and Jeremy before we tackle anything else?"

"Yes, but—"

"Hi," Jake said as he walked into the foyer from the kitchen. He looked up the stairs, then at his two guests. "Is she all right?"

He'd been up there twice when Destiny was with Divinity, although it was obvious Divinity was fine. But Destiny couldn't laugh at his anxiety. "You're a very nervous father-to-be."

Jake tried to smile. "I'm doing better." He frowned. "She's delicate."

Destiny laughed then. "Like a Belgian work-horse?"

"Not funny." But Jake's smile appeared. "Stay for dinner." He was already halfway up the stairs.

"Another time," Brace answered. "We have to take our two swimming."

Jake nodded but didn't pause in his ascension. "Children need care," he said, the words fading as he hurried to the library.

Brace held the door for her, and they walked outside to where Dorothy and Pepper Lally were entertaining the children.

Longtime residents of Yokapa County, the couple, who'd married late in life, seemed unflappable. Destiny had liked them at first meeting shortly after her arrival.

Dorothy looked their way, then walked over to them. "I've got to warn you. You could have a fight on your hands if you want to adopt Ella and Jeremy. Not because that buzzard Clyde Smoot cares about these two, but he can smell money like a hound dog scents a kill. I know the Smoots. Most of them are lazy, and that includes Clyde. He's also mean, greedy, and stupid." She glanced at the children, then back at Destiny and Brace. "Their mother was a Durham, good people. Why she ever hooked up with Clyde Smoot when her husband Tom died, I don't know. She probably didn't either. She was too soft. He played on her feelings, I've no doubt. After her death he kept the kids around so he could collect the insurance money coming from their mother and belonging to them."

Dorothy shook her head. "I tried more than once to do something, but I was shut out. You seem to have the power to get things done." She cleared her throat. "I'm known for being blunt, so I'll tell you straight out. Don't play games with those two children. Too much at stake."

Destiny felt the blood rise in her face. "I wouldn't do that—"

"Neither would I," Brace said. "We want what's best for them. They've improved in less than a week."

"I took them to the doctor the other day," Destiny added. "They're healthy, although since I haven't been able to track down any medical records, they both need to get all their vaccinations."

"Fine," Dorothy said. "But I'm not talking about how you're caring for them. I'm talking about negative emotions and tension. Get rid of them."

Destiny bristled, then buckled. "You're right, of course."

Dorothy looked at Brace, who nodded, grim visaged. "Good," Dorothy said. "Take them home, then."

Destiny was glad the children chattered all the way to Brace's car. She counted it a coup that their outfits, haircuts, and cleanliness had given them a different outlook on life. It went beyond soap, food, and clothes. There was almost a sense of contentment in them. They were more forthcoming, though their eyes could still darken with shadows. There wasn't a quick way to dissolve their fears. She had mixed feelings about Brace's commitment to them, his growing closeness to the two. It was painful for her to be with him, but she wouldn't do anything to shatter his friendship with the children.

She should've been an actress, she thought, then she might be more comfortable in the multiple roles she was playing. Keeping the children at ease demanded she avoid confrontations with Brace, though she itched to battle him on more than one front.

She wanted Brace, if anything, more than ever. It made her ill to think of losing him, yet she knew she couldn't go back to the way things had been, to the way they'd lived. How could she accept his blatant infidelity? That still was a raw wound. Distrust could smother love. She didn't want the slow disintegration of all that had been good between them. Wasn't a clean break best? She'd had to leave him once. It made her ill to contemplate another parting—

"What are you thinking?" he asked as he started driving along the curving drive of The Arbor.

It would've been easier to hedge, dissemble, to play with words as they'd so often done. Nuts! She had to face facts. If she didn't get some of it out in the open, it would continue to fester. The children were bright enough to sense division. Their instincts had been honed in a rough school. "Mostly about you," she said.

He sent her a wary look. "Oh?"

"Yes." She turned to glance at the back seat before continuing. The children were engrossed in one of the car games Brace had produced for them. "You've caused a problem by coming here, Brace. I think we'd better thrash that out, and soon."

Hands gripping the wheel of the Jaguar, he nodded. "When and where?"

"Today. No, tonight. Take me out to dinner. I'll ask Dorothy to babysit."

"Fine."

They didn't say anything more until they reached the condominium.

"Are we going sailing?" Jeremy asked, his voice and expression revealing that he expected them to say no.

"Sure," Brace said. "You and Ella go with Destiny and get changed. I'll meet you out front." He grinned when the boy beamed at him.

Jeremy and Ella raced across the tarmac toward the bridge leading to Destiny's unit.

Destiny looked at Brace. "That was nice. They haven't had much fun or many good times."

Brace hauled in a deep breath. "We can change that."

She shook her head, her heart banging against her chest wall. She wanted to throw herself in his arms and never leave. "Can't. I won't live that way again."

His hands fisted. "You need to listen to me, Des. There's nothing on earth we can't make better."

"I've listened to you, too many times. The metamorphosis shouldn't be mine."

"Dammit, Destiny, you know I'll do anything—"

She put up her hand, cutting him off. "Some things can't be changed, namely the past. Your life and the way you live it are ingrained in you and the rest of that rat pack who inhabit what you call a social life. Maybe if you hadn't been so caught up in it—"

"Destiny, I have never been unfaithful to you—"

"So you told me before I left California. Those pictures didn't lie, though. That woman works in your office—"

"Worked. Past tense. I don't know how that was set up, but that's what it was. You know pictures can be doctored. It happens all the time."

She swallowed, keeping her voice as low as his. "Yes, I know that. I also recognized the silk tie that was the only bit of clothing you were wearing. I gave it to you."

"Yes," he said through his teeth. "There's a lot I can't explain. I also realize that my family can be cold—"

"They were interested in my stocks, shares, bonds, construction company, and computer outfit, ad infinitum, ad nauseam, nothing else. I got sick of it, that and the lifestyle. The pictures were the last straw, Brace. We should've gotten to know each other better before we married. Maybe then we wouldn't have bothered." Every word was like a nail in her chest. It tore her apart to say anything that could cause an irreparable wound, but she needed to tell him.

White faced, he glanced at her. "I know it was quick. I've never regretted it. I'm sorry about this mess. I mean that." He pulled the key from the ignition.

She got out of the car.

"Are you coming, Destiny?" Jeremy called.

"Right away." She walked away from Brace without another word.

"I'm not giving up."

His words seemed to float out on the lake breeze, then whirl around her as she followed the children to her condo. They had already disappeared around the path.

She hurried, not hearing anything more from Brace or the children. "Hey, you two, are you hiding on—" She rounded the corner to their front door and stopped in her tracks.

A huge man, over six feet tall and bearded, with a large beer gut hanging over his belt, gripped both children by the nape. Their faces were twisted with pain and fear. Not a sound issued from them.

"You must be Clyde." Destiny tried to stay calm. The galoot could break their necks with one twist of those huge hands. She'd handled people like him, but never when it involved children she'd come to love. *Concentrate! Remember your training.*

"Yeah. Clyde Smoot. Now get outta the way. I'm takin' my kids outta here. Course, now that I've seen what a hot-lookin' broad you are, I might come back and give you a little—"

"Shut up," Destiny said through her teeth, anger welling like a hurricane in her throat.

"Nobody talks to—"

"Release them, or I'll have you put away for the

rest of your life. I'm not playing games with you. The authorities know—"

"They don't know crap, and neither do you, fancy lady. I'm taking these two with me. You don't get outta the way, I'll go through you. They's money to me, and you ain't gettin' in the way of it."

"Take your hands off them." Destiny was sure she could stop him long enough for the children to get free and run. She could get in at least one good hit. "Children, get ready to—"

Still gripping the children by the necks, he growled and charged.

Destiny grabbed at the closest porch stanchion, turning her body. She swung her legs high, thrusting her feet like a punch. She caught him square in the chest, only staggering him. It was enough to make him release the children.

"Run!" Destiny ordered. They did.

"You bitch, you think you—"

Destiny felt Brace like the wind at her side, then the two men collided like battering rams. She looked around her, desperate for a weapon. Brace had studied karate, but she feared he was no match for the barrel-chested Clyde and his long reach. Just as she thought that, Clyde was slammed to the ground.

He rolled to his feet just as fast.

Wide-eyed, Destiny spotted the gardener's hoe, steel edged with an oak handle. It had to be her weapon of choice. Hefting it, she turned and swung, catching Clyde right after he'd landed a haymaker on Brace. Anger had given her impetus, years of training provided the expertise. She struck with all her might on the back of his neck, almost breaking the implement.

Clyde's howls of rage and pain scattered crows from the nearby trees. He whirled on her, ready to charge, when Jeremy ran at him and sank his little incisors into the fleshy part of Clyde's calf.

Clyde bent to grab the boy, but Brace got Jeremy out of the way first, then slammed his fist into Clyde's gut. The whush of anger and surprise pouring out of the intruder raised angry gulls from the water.

Destiny brought the hoe down again on the back of his head, sending the reeling Goliath to his face. "Now I'm going to teach you not to strike children," she said, bringing the hoe back over her shoulder.

Brace grasped her wrist, stopping the downward swing. "Don't. You could kill him with that."

"Good plan," she said, grim faced, angrier than she'd ever been.

Brace chuckled, then winced, cradling his jaw in one hand. "It's a good one, but forget it. These kids need you here more than they need to be visiting you in jail. He'll be handled." He turned his head. "I hear sirens."

"I called p'lice. I know how—nine-one-one," Ella said, tears in her eyes.

"Darling," Destiny said, dropping her weapon. "He can't hurt you, and you won't go with him. I won't let anyone take you and Jeremy." She hugged the little girl, turning her away from the behemoth who was trying to rise.

"Don't get up," Brace told Clyde. "If you do, she won't have the chance to finish you. I'll do it."

Moaning, Clyde sank back, his face pressed into the ground.

In a flurry of activity the sheriff arrived, with Jake Blessing right behind him.

"What's going on?" Jake asked. "Darnell heard your call on the police radio. Divinity's upset," he added as though he'd just announced a 7.7 earthquake.

"Sorry," Destiny said, and gave him the bare bones of what had occurred, while Brace did the same with the sheriff. "He got nasty," she finished.

Jake's smile was tight. "He's been living in one of the apartment buildings I own. He's just been evicted."

"I'm pressing charges," Destiny and Brace said at the same time.

Jake grinned. "Glad you're agreeing on something. I'm out of here, then."

Destiny nodded, not looking at Brace.

When the sheriff left, taking Clyde with him, she turned to Brace. "I—I don't think we—"

"We should and we will."

"You don't know what I was going to say." She frowned at him.

"Sure I do. You were going to come up with another reason for us not to share parenting. Face it, Des. Your arguments won't work. I'm not leaving.

I'm here with you and I'm staying. What does it take to make you see the light? We love each other—"

"We did."

"Do. Things went wrong, but not with us. Too many outsiders dictated to us. Nothing will do that anymore, if we don't let it. The two of us shouldn't be the most difficult part of this, Des."

For a long moment they stared at each other.

Myriad emotions warred in her. It was as though she'd lost gravity and was floating around in a cloud of indecision. Relief and joy welled before she had a chance to be angry. He'd been with her for almost a week now. That was longer than they'd been together when they first married. Of course, back then their time had been spent quite differently.

The years since then had been dotted with disagreements on a variety of subjects, including her family, his family, his money and hers, where she should work, what their goals should be, individually and together. She had finally realized she couldn't operate as a part-time wife, part-time executive, part-time pacifier. Living as a third of this or that had been too fragmenting. The coup de grace had been the pictures she'd gotten in the mail a month earlier, proving Brace had another life. She hadn't been able to listen to his denials, or accept the ones she'd heard.

Blinking, she reentered the world around her. Taking a deep breath, she studied Brace. "I can't throw you out." As though she wanted that!

"Right. Besides, I have my own place next door."

"You saved the children." She blinked. "Oh, your jaw! I'll get some ice."

"You were pretty good yourself." He smiled at her. "If I'd known you had such a wicked swing, I would've signed us up for the Gold golf tournaments at the club."

A reluctant laugh escaped her. "I was angry."

"No kidding."

His slow smile made her knees weak. "You were wonderful with Clyde."

"So were you." His grin twisted. "We're still a team, Destiny."

She could only stare at him, out of breath, heart pounding. "Not according to the papers I signed."

"I know." He looked toward the lake. "We need to talk, but Jeremy wants to sail."

"So why don't we go sailing?" Jeremy asked, appearing at their sides. "Clyde's gone."

The adults looked down at him as though he'd spoken in a foreign language.

Ella pulled on the hem of Destiny's shorts. "You said we would."

"Ah, yes, I did." She hauled in air as though there was a limited supply. "Jeremy, Ella, you were very brave. I know you were frightened, but you showed a great deal of courage."

Ella's thumb went to her mouth, her shy smile fitting around it.

Jeremy looked down, then up again. "I knew he'd hurt you."

Destiny put a hand on each of their heads. "Yes,

he would have. Cowards have the knack for it." As she looked down at them, a strong purpose struggled to the surface. She was going to fight for them. "We're going to keep Clyde away."

"There are people who will help us do that," Brace said, then he grinned. "Did somebody mention sailing?"

The children grinned back and nodded.

It was on the tip of Destiny's tongue to tell him this didn't include him, that this was a part of *her* life. She'd been cut out of so much of Brace's. What kept her quiet, she didn't know. She only nodded. "Let's do it."

The children whooped while her heart thumped. They were acting like a family. No! It was crazy! *Don't let hope take over, fool.*

"Trust me, Destiny."

Brace had moved up behind her, his voice shivering over her. She swallowed. "You might be asking too much. We've disappointed each other."

"No! I've made mistakes with you, but you've never disappointed me."

She tried to smile. "You were going to make a call."

FOUR

The days seemed to sweep through their lives like zephyrs. There was a great deal to do every day, including the many legal steps they needed to take to protect the children.

Brace always seemed to be at her condo, taking care of the children while she took care of business, and joining them when they played. Sailing, dining out, walking, laughing. They did it all, just like that intimate grouping called family.

Destiny was caught between joy and fear, recklessness and caution. Negative and positive thoughts bounced off her as quickly as the choppy lake water hit the shore.

Swimming had become her analgesic. She swam every day, stroking hard, arms and legs pumping, to bring a salubrious effect. Diving deep into the clear green water and watching the undulating weeds was calming and cleansing to her frayed nerves. Wishing

Brace to another planet and wanting him at her side at the same time was doing a job on her mental equilibrium.

What should have been the most galling was that despite Brace's daily presence, she didn't feel threatened. Maybe a tad coerced, but she was willing to overlook that. Being together with the children was a subtle balm, bringing about a soothing sense of companionship.

What had bothered her most in her marriage had been the growing feeling of isolation, the sense that she and Brace traveled in parallel lines, rarely touching. Their new alliance wasn't like that. Alliance? Relationship? Was that what it was? she wondered. Better to name it pandemonium, the poet Milton's own made-up word for the circus of demons in his writings. The two children had brought a delightful chaos into her life, a warming messiness that she'd never known. For better or worse, Brace had become a part of that picture.

Such was Destiny's concentration one afternoon as she swam that she didn't notice the whirring sound, the far-off hiss and growl of an engine that grew louder every second. As the water became more agitated, roiling below the surface, she lifted her head. A boat was in her vicinity. Glancing around, she threw herself upward, straining to see. It wasn't a good idea to be in the path of a speeding boat. They might not spot her. As though it had risen from the depths, she saw the prow of a speedboat heading right at her. She yelled but her voice was no match for the roar of the motor.

Damn! Doubling her body, she snapped downward in a steep dive. Deeper and deeper, reaching for the bottom, she knifed toward the weeds, seeking the protection of the depths. Her chest expanded with the pressure, hurting as she fought to stay under. Seeing spots before her eyes, she knew she was pressing her luck as she angled toward shore, trying not to surface.

Spiking upward at last, she shot through the surface, gasping for air, pushing back her goggles. For a moment she saw nothing. Then a hand, then another, both bathed in the glow of the bright sunlight, were there. They grasped her, holding tight. Blinking, Destiny looked up into blurred faces, cast into deep shadow by the sun behind them. "Who—?"

"Take our hands. Hurry. Hold on." Two people spoke at the same time. One man? One woman?

She couldn't be sure who they were, but she reached out, feeling herself being lifted out of the water as though she weighed no more than a feather. She seemed to fly through the air, then settle on top of one of the many deep-water rafts scattered offshore.

Taken aback at the near miss, she shook her head, then cupped her hand over her eyes, trying to see. Was the boat speeding away a "cigarette," one of the powerful speedboats more at home in the ocean than on a lake? The craft was all but out of sight. There was nothing to see but frothy wake and a hazy proba-

bility that the color of the boat could have been gold
or cream.

"Thank y—" Destiny turned to speak to her rescuers, but she was alone on the raft. The slapping
waves made it undulate beneath her. She scrutinized
the surrounding water. Nothing. No one. Two people had helped her. Where were they? Why had they
gone? How had they reached her so fast?

Had it been a man and a woman? Even without a
clear view she was sure it had been.

She glanced all around again, then slid back into
the water, stroking hard for shore, her mind churning with what had occurred.

When she felt herself caught around the waist
and lifted up, she swallowed water. "Wha—?"

"It's all right, darling. I have you. Damn, I
thought he'd hit you." Brace clasped her close to his
chest, towing her to shallow water.

"I . . . I can—"

"Shh, it's all right. That son of a bitch almost got
you." When he found his footing, he lifted her, carrying her to shore, clasping her tight. Not releasing
her, he caught up a towel and swaddled it around
her. "I have to get you warm." He scooped up a
T-shirt and pulled it over her. Then he urged her
down onto another towel. "Stay still."

"Those people," she said. "Where did they go?"

"What people? As far as I could tell, there was
just the driver in the boat. I think it was a man."
Brace ground his teeth. "And if I ever get—"

"No, not that one. The people who pulled me to the raft."

He shook his head. "I missed that. I only saw you, and that bastard almost on top of you."

"Oh. I wanted to thank them." She shivered, gazing out at the water. "I—I had the feeling I'd met them somewhere."

"For now let's get you warm and dry." He sat down next to her, slipping his arm around her. "Better?"

She nodded, a part of her wondering about her rescuers, the rest of her responding to Brace. "You didn't see anyone?"

"Just the boat and you." He looked out over the lake. "I'll know that craft again. After I get you inside and settled, I'll talk to the sheriff."

"Thanks . . . thanks."

He inched even closer to her, both arms around her now. "That scared the hell out of me."

Silence stretched between them like a frayed rubber band, popping when he spoke.

"I thought he'd hit you," he said against her hair.

She nodded, her wet hair rubbing his chest. "So did I."

"I'll come swimming with you from now on."

She smiled, looking up at him. "I swim all the time, and nothing's happened before. It was just some wave jockey doing his rooster tails. Showing off is a universal game."

He studied her. "Not all males think it's a good idea to play nasty tricks."

She returned his stare. "I know that."

"Des, let's not throw it away." He kissed her forehead. "Please, let's give it another chance. We can't afford to toss our lives in the sewer without trying."

She took a deep breath. "Sounds good, Brace. Don't get me wrong. I wanted to save us . . . but I think it's too late. Our families know about the break. We've more or less settled on it—"

"I haven't."

She went on. "Even if you and I come to an agreement, there's always our families. Neither have ever approved of our marriage."

"My family likes you better than you know."

She shook her head. "Blind faith on your part, I'm afraid. Your family against mine was like the Confederacy and the Union. Not a good mix. Reason goes out the window. We were caught in the middle with no turning room. I'm not sure I could go through it again." She pulled back a fraction. "What we had wasn't resilient or strong enough to—"

"What we had was great, Des. Maybe we didn't handle things right, but don't denigrate what we had. It was beautiful."

She bit her lip. "Isn't it better to have a clean break, than to do a slow waltz from dislike, to disgust, to the eventual shattering?" She shook her head again. "Too much pain." Inside she was screaming that she didn't want to be parted from him. When he'd shown up on her doorstep the day she'd found

Jeremy and Ella, it had been an answer to a prayer she hadn't even realized she'd made. To separate from him again would be a new agony.

"Let's change us," he said. "We can work on that. We're worth it, Des. The hell with the rest of them."

"Easy to say, not to do." She wanted it so much, it hurt.

"I'm willing to try. How about you?"

"We . . . I have the children. It's a big responsibility. I can't carve myself into two directions at this point. Not when it's so important to Ella and Jeremy."

"All right. I agree they need help. We've talked about this. I think two heads are better than one. What do you say to a pact? The kids need our concentration. We put us aside for the time being and deal with Ella and Jeremy in the best possible way."

"Brace, I signed the papers."

"I didn't. Now isn't the time. You said that yourself. You don't want to parcel yourself at such a crucial time for the children. What do you say? Truce?" He shifted to hold out his right hand to her.

She hesitated.

"Take a chance," he whispered.

For several heartbeats she didn't move. Then she nodded, once, twice, and grasped his hand.

"Good." He kissed her on the cheek, then pressed her hand to his chest. "Just thought you'd like to know how your answer affected me."

The pounding under her fingers had her own

blood climbing into warp speed, her pulse fluttering like a teenager's on her first date. All the pent-up feelings she had for him crashed through her like a flash flood. It was like being dropped off a cliff. Being with Brace was dangerous. Breathtaking. Exciting. "We—we need to keep perspective."

"Right." He pulled her to her feet. "We need to get you into the shower. Tonight I'll cook."

Warily she eyed him. "Not one of those awful Boy Scout dinners you used to prepare, I hope, with everything thrown into foil and shoved into the oven."

"I've improved." He laughed at her obvious skepticism. "Trust me."

As though a fist had landed in her chest, she was immobilized and breathless.

For long moments they stared at each other.

He inhaled a shaky breath, one finger tracing a line on her bare arm. "I know what you're thinking. 'Trust' is a tough word in our vocabulary. Ours has been dented. Can't deny it. We have to do some shoring up."

"Sounds like a big project." She couldn't keep the tremolo from her voice.

"We'll put a time limit on it. Okay?" He wrapped the two towels around her and turned her toward the stairs leading up to the condo.

"How do we do that?" Her voice was as low as his.

"As I said. We work for the children, then on our agenda. Maybe we salvage it all. We cooperate. Bury the nasty incidents." She stiffened under his arm. "If we don't, let's say, after five weeks, feel things are on an upswing, then we look at alternatives."

Destiny swallowed. That would mean parting. Did she have the guts to do that again? It made her insides turn to jelly to think of it.

"We can only try."

His whisper coiled around her, heating her. Her nod of agreement was as unconscious and deeply imbedded as the need to have hope, not just in Brace, but in the future. Her world had narrowed when she'd left him. Now it was expanding again. Could she handle it?

They were silent when they entered her condo.

Brace scanned the great room. "Where are Jeremy and Ella?"

"Mrs. Duggan ran them over to the tutor's. When Mrs. D is through shopping, she'll bring them home."

"Good plan. She's quite a lady."

"Yes, she is. Divinity recommended her as just a cleaning woman, but I feel like she's taken charge of the whole household. She likes the children. That's her biggest recommendation."

"Right. Would you like to use the hot tub?"

"No, I'll shower." She moved past him on trembling legs, entered the bathroom, shut and locked the door.

She stripped off her bathing suit and stepped into the steaming spray of the shower. As she washed her hair, she recalled the two people who had helped her when the speeding boat had almost run her down. Who were they? Their voices and features had been blurred. Yet she could've sworn she'd heard those voices before. How had they gotten to her so quickly? Where had they gone?

She had dried her hair, lightly applied makeup, and was half-dressed when she heard a sudden scurrying and flurry of noise. Ella and Jeremy were back. Mrs. Duggan would've seen them to the door, then left for the day.

Fastening her walking shorts, she grimaced. Were her hips widening? Probably. She left the bedroom, promising to get herself a smaller mirror. When she walked down the hall to the kitchen, her hips and everything else emptied from her mind.

Her kitchen looked like a war zone. Brace's idea of preparing a meal called for every pan and container in the house. The countertop was littered with assorted flatware, plates, pans, and utensils.

Destiny leaned against the doorjamb, caught between laughter and dismay. Studying the trio in the throes of the wildest food preparation since the Mad Hatter's tea party, she didn't have to wonder why Mrs. Duggan had left in such a hurry. No doubt she thought Brace was demented.

"Now, wait, wait," Brace was cautioning the children. "We have to see if you light the oven first or put the food in cold. I'm not certain, but I think that's an important point. What does it say in the book, Jeremy?"

Destiny eyed the boy with his tongue caught between his teeth, squinting at the open cookbook. She could sense his reading skills were limited. She didn't make a sound.

"I . . . I think it says to heat first. Pre . . . heat, it says." He looked up, relieved when Brace went to the stove and fiddled with the oven dial. "Don't you know how to do it, Brace?"

"Give me a minute, will you? These are infernal machines designed to give men grief."

Ella grinned. "It's easy. I can do it. We had to cook Clyde's food." A shadow, like a pulled shade, crossed her face.

Brace kissed her. "Clyde is too stupid to know how wonderful you are."

Ella grinned up at him and nodded.

Strange how priorities could change, Destiny thought as she studied the confusion in front of her. The sight of the three of them together struck a chord in her being, touched feelings so deep, she hadn't even known they resided there. Not even her emotion-filled career had dredged up such an amalgam of feelings. Protectiveness and nurturing flooded her.

"Now, let's see," Brace said. "Salad. We should be able to do that. Simple, huh?" He looked at the children, who looked unsure.

"Clyde ate hamburgers with the blood showing," Jeremy said.

Ella nodded. "The ashes from his cigarettes used to drop on them. He ate those too."

"An epicure, by gum," Brace observed, earning

grins from his counterparts. He pawed through the refrigerator, finding escarole, parsley, peppers, and celery. He spied the tomatoes on the windowsill and sniffed them. "Umm, they smell good. I'll bet they came from one of the farms around here." He put his raw materials on the counter and ran cold water into a deep dish. "I think this should be salt water to wash away germs," he told the children.

Kneeling on the stools on the other side of the island that contained the sink, stove, and a wide area for work, they watched him.

Destiny decided to let them muddle through the meal. Their bonding was so apparent, so strong.

"Let's see. I think because it's summer we don't have to peel the tomatoes." Brace grimaced. "I hope I'm right. It would save time." He washed the vegetables and put them into a collander, then swiped his hands down the apron he'd tied around his waist.

"What can we do?" Jeremy asked.

"Ah, hands washed. Right?"

"You saw us wash," Ella reminded him.

"Okay. This will be a community salad. I'll cut the veggies. Jeremy, you tear the escarole. Ella, you arrange the stuff in those bowls." He pointed to each thing in turn.

"I wonder if I'll like this," Ella mused.

"Of course you will. Rabbits worldwide will be jealous of your salad."

The child giggled.

Destiny was enthralled with the salad makers. Her eyes stung as she saw Brace open his mouth and test one of the pepper chunks offered by Jeremy. Finally she stepped forward. "Could I make the dressing?"

Three smiles turned her way along with three nods. "Umm, everything smells good." She glanced at the omelet pan and saw the smoke, so she turned the heat down as she crossed to the fridge in one smooth movement. She decided on a sweetish, not too tart dressing of brown sugar, vinegar, and a little oil. She chopped basil and oregano into the mix, then leaned against the counter to study the operation. "What're we having?"

"Fru-eetta . . . I think," Jeremy said. "It's got eggs and potatoes and smells good."

"Ah. Frittata."

Three expressions went on hold as they waited for her reaction.

"Just what I wanted."

Three beaming faces looked relieved.

Destiny laughed.

Dinner was good. The frittata seemed enhanced by its too brown bottom. The bread, warmed to piping hot in the oven, was sourdough and crusty, freshly made by Dorothy Lally that morning. Cold milk was the beverage. Destiny ate everything on her plate, something she hadn't done in some time.

They cleared the table, stuffed the dishwasher, started it, and went out to the terrace to play dominoes. The children had become intrigued with the ancient game.

The evening seemed to fly. After the children

were put to bed, Destiny wandered back outside, leaning on the deck railing, studying the star-filled sky.

"The Big Dipper looks close enough to touch," Brace said at her side.

She straightened, her defenses rising as fast as the heat that bubbled through her each time he was close. "Yes."

"Will you ever let me explain about those pictures, Des?"

She looked to the north, away from him. "Probably not."

"You've always been a fair person. Didn't it occur to you that the photos could have been doctored?"

"Yes. It might've had more relevance if I hadn't seen you kissing Wendy Carradine at the club."

He was silent for a long time. "I was a fool. She kept coming on to me, I'd had too much to drink, and I was angry with you for some stupid reason I can't even remember now."

"In other words, just because."

"Yes."

"I'll bet that's a first as far as reasons go for adultery."

"Stop! I wasn't unfaithful to you."

He hadn't moved, but it felt as though he'd surrounded her with himself. Rage, hurt, a desire to lash out, all those responses she'd thought under control bubbled up in her. "Of course you weren't. Besides, adultery is such a mundane reason for separating."

"Sarcasm doesn't get us anywhere, Des."

"No? Well, I feel like being that way. You drove a hole through everything I held dear." She whirled around, jabbing her index finger at him. "You took over my corporation because you thought you could handle it better than I—"

"You wanted that—"

"—and you practically chose all our friends. Most of them unmitigated bores, by the way—"

"There are some decent people on this planet who don't feel they need to save the world every day."

"And there are those, not so good, who don't give a tinker's damn about anyone but themselves, and consider those less endowed something to be scraped off a shoe."

"Not all."

"I didn't fit in with your family." She inhaled a shaky breath. "We don't fit, Brace. Good night." She left him there, staring out at the lake.

Hot tears scalded her cheeks before she slammed the bedroom door behind her. Sobs were smothered by a bath towel. Finally she washed her face, brushed her teeth, and went to bed. She didn't fall asleep until just before dawn.

Three days after the contretemps with Brace, Destiny drove across Yokapa County to the medical building adjacent to General Hospital. Divinity would be there, getting a checkup with an obstetrician. They hoped to have a coffee or tea—decaffeinated, of course—somewhere after her appointment, along with another friend of Divinity's, Dynasty Jones. Since the arrival of Jeremy and Ella she hadn't seen as much of Divinity as she would've liked, though they talked on the phone nearly every day. She'd left the house early, taking the children to their tutor for their daily session. She hadn't seen Brace. Maybe he'd gone back to California. She'd more or less told him to go. Her chest knotted with hurt. *Think of something else.*

A fleeting glance in the rearview mirror showed the black car. She'd seen it before when she'd turned onto the main highway leading toward the hospital. Had it been behind her on the country roads she'd traveled to the highway? Fanciful. She was too used to seeing pickup trucks on the roads. A car was an anomaly.

Spying the medical complex, she turned into the parking lot, locked the car, and ambled toward the emergency room entrance. Divinity had told her that was the quickest way to the attached building where many of the doctors had their offices.

Another person was behind her, so she held the door. As she did she saw the rear of a black car as it passed the building. She shivered. She was getting too imaginative.

After getting the room number from the hospital directory, she took the elevator to the third floor. A nurse directed her to a room down the hall. Divinity was in the waiting room. "The doctor running late?"

"Not really. He wanted to do a little blood work

along with some other tests." She rolled her eyes. "This baby stuff is complicated. Sorry it's taking so long."

Destiny laughed, glancing at her watch. "Don't worry about it. I'm relieved you're in good shape. We can do the coffee thing another time. Where's Dynasty?"

"She's in the ladies' room." Even as she spoke, Dynasty entered the room.

Destiny had met Dynasty not long after arriving in Yokapa County. She'd been impressed with Divinity's friend, who seemed very forthright and kind. Dynasty owned a horse farm in the area, though she and her husband, Aaron Burcell spent part of the year in Kentucky at his family-owned horse farm. Divinity had told Destiny that the Burcell farm had raised and trained some of the top thoroughbreds in racing, including a few Kentucky Derby winners.

"Hi, Destiny," Dynasty said. "At least we can sit here and chat."

Destiny laughed. "Great. My only schedule involves the children. I want to be home when Mrs. Duggan brings them back from the tutor's."

For almost an hour the three women chatted.

Twice Divinity was taken away by the nurse, then returned.

"I should get going," Destiny said reluctantly. She'd had such a good time. "Is there anything you need before I leave?"

"Maybe some water while I'm waiting," Divinity

said. "There's a kitchenette about two doors down the hall."

Destiny nodded. "I'll get it and come back in a minute."

Wandering down the hall, she studied different closed doors, finally choosing what she hoped was the right one. It wasn't—she'd found a linen storage room—but there was a sink and paper cup dispenser. She was reaching for a cup when voices behind the high utility shelves that held neat stacks of linen stopped her.

"We take this Smith dame when she comes along the hall?" a man said, his voice rough and guttural.

"No, fool." Another man spoke, his voice sharper, harsh. "We watch that doctor's waiting room. She's in there with her friends. We keep on the whites, then take her in the elevator. We put her in the laundry cart and wheel it right out the emergency entrance. Boom, she disappears. Nobody knows. We get paid."

"Do we kill her?"

"Probably."

Destiny listened, incredulous. They had to be discussing her. She lowered her hand, eying the door behind her.

"How do we know when she comes out of there?" the first man asked.

"We watch, stupid. In case we miss, there're windows all along the end corridor that face on the parking lot. Herb will be watching from the car. Now let's get out of here before someone comes in and questions us."

Hearing the two men move toward the door, Destiny edged around a white cabinet to hide, holding her breath. She peeked around it when she heard the almost silent swish of the door. They were gone! She'd have to go out the same way if there was no other exit. She looked around, not moving from her spot for fear of making noise and bringing them back into the room.

When she saw the huge dumbwaiter on the far wall, she grimaced. Not an escape vehicle of choice, but she had no other. She crept over to the conveyance, eased herself into it, and pulled down the door.

It slogged down its shaft in slow, bumping progress. When it stopped, she raised the cover and steam met her. Apparently she was in the laundry. Slipping out, she stayed still for a long moment, gazing around her.

Sets of the white pants and pullovers worn by the hospital orderlies were neatly folded in a laundry cart. She jerked a pair on over her clothes, then went to find a way out.

The first door she found led into the hospital. On the adjacent wall was another door that opened into the parking lot nearest the emergency room entrance. Cautiously looking around, she spotted a black car. She'd swear it was the one that had followed her. The driver was in it, and he seemed to be looking in the direction of her own parked car.

Her brain tumbled over possible solutions to her

problem. Taking a deep breath, she went to a wall phone and dialed 911.

As soon as the operator answered, she explained where she was and what she'd overheard, and gave the plate number of the black car and a description of the driver. After she replaced the receiver, she stayed where she was, counting the minutes. Had she heard a siren, or had she just hoped for one? When the interior door opened and an orderly entered the room, pushing a laundry cart filled with dirty bed-sheets, she decided she'd better go.

Outside, she distinctly heard sirens. As they came closer, she crept around a conveniently parked delivery truck, keeping the black car and the driver in her peripheral vision. She felt his glance, then knew it swung toward the two police cars blocking the parking lot exit.

Destiny slipped around one police car, stopping to stare along with the gathering crowd. She didn't know the driver of the black car. Why would he and his friends be after her?

Moving slowly, she turned and glanced toward the third floor of the medical building. She saw no faces in the windows. That didn't mean anything. They could be to one side, out of her sight. Still moving slowly, she crossed the parking lot, attempting to put herself beyond the building. She crouched as she reached the parked vehicles, weaving her way among them, heading for her own. When she reached her car, she edged up to see if anyone was watching her. She saw no one.

Scrambling into her car, she started it, backed out, and left the parking lot through the entrance, swerving around another car. Then she was on the side street, racing along too fast, anxious to get away. If they spotted her, she knew they'd follow her. But why were they after her?

It was like the old days, but she wasn't with the Bureau anymore, and there was no one who had a grudge against her, as far as she knew. She'd pushed somebody's buttons, though, and she'd better find out whose.

Hunched over the wheel, she had an odd sense of déjà vu. For the moment, it felt good to be taking action. She could handle herself. She'd been trained. Whoever was coming after her, for whatever reason, they'd find that out.

Easing back to just speedy, but not far enough over the limit to get nailed, she tore through the small city the hospital was in, one eye on the road ahead, the other on the rearview mirror. Had they intimated they'd kill her? Had to be a mistake.

She swung the car out of the side street onto the main road, to the blare of horns at her back. Was that a black car in the distance behind her? Speeding through a yellow light, she did a ninety-degree left turn back off the highway, deciding to take the narrow country roads home.

She didn't lessen her speed, though some of the ravines on either side were large enough to swallow a tractor trailer. Swinging out onto the lake road on a hard right turn, she leaned over the wheel. Whatever the hell was going on, she'd get to the bottom of it.

She saw the beginning of the large cove that fronted the condo property, then the driveway. She slowed, but not much. Wheeling into the drive, she sent up a shower of stones, bringing crows cawing in protest from the pines. Tires screeching, she roared into the parking lot as though she were a top finisher at Indy. She slammed on the brakes, skidded sideways, and stopped. She laid her head on the wheel, taking deep breaths. She mustn't look frazzled when she entered the condo. The children had had enough madness in their lives.

The driver's door was flung open. Brace was there, lifting her from the car. "What the hell is going on? What's wrong? Tell me."

She looked up at him, intending to put him off because the truth was so farfetched. "Men. I heard them talking in the medical center. They were after me."

Brace's eyes narrowed, then he looked down the drive. "Come on." He would've carried her, but she pushed back, shaking her head.

"I can handle it."

Once in the condo, he locked the door, then followed her to the breakfast bar. "I need to make a call. Tell me what happened."

Destiny told him what she'd done as she moved around the kitchen making tea.

He snatched up the telephone. His message was brief and harsh—Destiny was in danger. He replaced

the receiver, then eyed her over the separator between kitchen and living area.

"Tea will be ready in a minute," she said.

"Right," he said through his teeth.

"Jeremy and Ella?"

"Over at the Burcell farm, learning to ride. Mrs.
Duggan took them over at Jake's and Aaron's re-
quests."

Destiny smiled and nodded. Then she leaned
back and sipped her tea. She watched as he went to
the phone again.

"Did you know them?" he asked before he dialed.

She shook her head. While he talked, she sat at
the kitchen table and finished the tea. After he was
done, he walked into the kitchen and put his arms
around her. She didn't struggle.

"I didn't imagine it," she said.

"I never thought you did."

"I can't figure it out, dammit. Whatever's going
on, they're not intimidating me."

"No one's going to hurt you. I'll see to that."

"You believe me."

"Of course I do. And I'm proud of you. You don't
buckle under threats and intimidation and you have
courage. You proved that when you worked for the
Bureau, and when you married me." He kissed her
hair. She moved her head, though she didn't free
herself.

"The telephone calls?" she asked.

He hesitated. "First I called Jake's friend Darnell. Then I called Webb."

"Your security man at Mendez-Coolidge?"

"Yes. He and some of his people are on the way. We need to talk to the sheriff too." He leaned back so he could see her face. "I trust your friend Jake, and his people, but they're busy, he has a business. I want people around you who will focus completely on you."

She didn't point out that he was every bit as busy as Jake Blessing with his own business to run.

"Take a rest," he said. "I'll stay with you." When her mouth snapped shut on a yawn and her eyes narrowed in suspicion, he laughed. "Your virtue is safe, ma'am. You have my word."

"Very funny," she muttered, relieved that he'd be at her side, annoyed that he didn't push to make love with her. Forget that, she told herself. For now she needed some rest. Then she'd be armed and ready for whatever came.

FIVE

The courtroom was silent after Divinity Blessing's impassioned closing statement.

The judge looked over his glasses, coughed, cleared his throat. "The court has studied these matters." His glance went from one lawyer to the other. "You have presented your suits admirably, and I've listened closely to your arguments." He rustled the papers in front of him. "I'd pretty much come to a decision after reading the records. It's cut and dried." He paused, coughed again. "The safety of the children, Ella and Jeremy Alcot-Durham, is the most important factor in this case. That, along with their continued health and happiness, has heavily influenced my decision. Also, their education under safe conditions will be mandated by this court. As a result of the information gained by this court, and the records from Social Services, Ella and Jeremy will be removed from the custody of Clyde Smoot."

He looked over his glasses, frowning when there was a murmur. "Since they've been in the care of John B. Coolidge and Destiny Smith Coolidge they have thrived, according to their tutor and Mrs. Coolidge's housekeeper. He pushed at the papers on his bench. "Mr. and Mrs. Coolidge have assured me that the care of children is a driving force in their lives and they will sue for permanent custody. Until that happens, they will remain in their care." He hit his gavel. "Dismissed."

Almost no one moved for a moment.

Then Clyde rose. "You ain't heard the last of this." He pointed at Destiny.

Brace surged to his feet. Jake's hand on his shoulder restrained him.

Destiny stared when Webb, the stolid security man from Mendez-Coolidge, leaned over the wooden barrier and tapped Clyde's shoulder, then whispered. The phlegmatic police guards simply watched.

Clyde whitened, then hurried from the courtroom.

"I hope he told him what he could do with his threats," Destiny muttered.

"I'm sure he did. Webb can be very articulate."

The icy humor in Brace's voice made her smile. "Thank you for going along with the judge about the children."

"We're married," Brace said curtly. "That means the children are ours. We have the obligation to give them comfort and joy. Right?"

She nodded. "But the divorce papers . . ."

"I've talked to Clint—"

"Evers?" He was Brace's lawyer and head of a very prestigious firm in California.

"Yes. He says we're still married, and that your papers can be discarded."

"I can't wait to hear what your family will say about that," she murmured.

"Mine? Wait until your family gets the news, and they will. They should arrive on your doorstep in no time. Since they can be heard through steel, I'm thinking of getting the wall between our condos re-inforced."

She grimaced. "I don't like to think about it, but if they all come, we'll need a hotel."

"That's what I figured. Jake offered another brace of condos he has, about a mile south of us and right on the lake."

They left the courtroom and walked along the wide corridor of the courthouse, the dark stained oak walls like a warm cape to the old building.

"Doesn't he have any property a little farther away?" Destiny asked.

"I'm afraid not, sweetheart, but I've told him to double the rent."

Mirth bubbled up in her. "My relatives will have a fit. They'll expect me to pick up the tab."

"So will mine. No way."

"It'll be war."

"Let 'em come. I've been itching for a good fight."

She stopped, one eyebrow arched. "Usually it was with me."

"Wrong. I never wanted to fight with you."

The huskiness in his voice heated her, turned her knees to pudding. "Then where did we go wrong? How did it get so far off track? Why did you need outside diversions?"

"I didn't," he ground out, his hands fisting.

"I have pictures," she shot back, though she wasn't as sure as she'd once been.

"Yes, dammit, and I can't explain that, but it isn't true."

They stared at each other, lost in the red emotion that had colored their life, especially in the last eighteen months. Issues seemed to mushroom, driving wedges between them. Even now, when they'd come to some sort of armistice because of the children, their bodies fairly hummed with negative vibrations.

"I can't go through that again," she said, agonized.

"Neither can I. Let's start fresh with the kids, as though life began the moment we met them. Let the past fade, and we'll wipe it from our lives." He spread his hands. "We have another shot. I want to take it, to start from square one."

Various emotions flitted over his face, challenging and hypnotizing her. "Big order," she said.

He nodded.

"We—we need ground rules."

Again his head jerked up and down, his hands still

flexing. "Right. No holding back. We discuss every-thing, every day. That's my first one. What's yours?"

"Take no calls or letters from anyone who wouldn't be supportive. There's been too much neg-ativity." She took a breath. "At least not while we're in this—this transitional period."

"Is that what it is?"

"I don't know. I don't have a better word."

As though the world had settled back around them, they looked at the passersby, then back at each other.

Destiny coughed. "We should leave this deal open-ended so we can amend it as necessary."

"For instance like banning our families." He held out his right hand.

She hesitated, then took a deep breath and shook it. "That should be tantamount to mounting a cam-paign in Siberia."

"Siberia would be simpler and warmer." When she laughed, he grinned and took her arm. "I feel better than I have in months."

She hesitated, then nodded.

Jeremy and Ella looked at them warily when they returned to Destiny's condo.

"It looks like you belong to us," she said simply. She didn't add that it could change, that there were steps to go through before anything could be final, not to mention the fragility of the relationship between Brace and herself. They'd take it one day at a time. That could be managed . . . somehow.

Neither child moved.

Destiny opened her mouth, then shut it again when she saw the single tear on Jeremy's cheek and the silent river of them on Ella's. Not able to stop her own weeping, she fell to her knees in front of them. "Oh, gosh, don't. We'll do well. See if we don't," she bubbled, clutching them. When she felt small, still too thin arms around her, she cried harder.

"Hey, you guys, you're causing a flood," Brace said, his own voice cracking. "We could be chased out of this place." He managed to scoop up the children and enclose Destiny in one motion. He put his head down to theirs. "It's going to work for us. You can put that in the bank."

Jeremy didn't smile, but his eyes brightened. "Maybe we should get a horse," he said. "Darnell says I've got a good seat."

Destiny stared at the boy, caught between amusement and amazement. "Well . . . it's a good idea, but we don't have the room yet, so we—"

"Miss Dynasty says she'll stable him," Jeremy said.

"She did?" Destiny answered, her voice faint. "My goodness, how . . . how sweet of her."

"We like her," Ella said.

"I'll bet," Destiny muttered. She shot a look at Brace when she felt him quiver. "Don't you laugh!"

"I'm not, I'm not, but I can assure you I'm definitely going to try to convince Jeremy he should join the family business in the future. He's an expert deal maker." He touched the boy's shoulder, then bit his lip as amusement overwhelmed him. "What's your family going to say if they see a menagerie?"

Destiny gave him an amused frown. "If they do arrive, they won't stay. Especially my aunt. Chaos offends her and sends her into a tizzy. One child, well cared for by others, was more than enough for her."

The arrested expression on her face had him nodding. "I see we're on the same wavelength. We need to get twenty more kids."

"That's a lot," Jeremy whispered.

"It certainly is," Destiny said. "Brace was making a joke because my aunt had only one child."

"Oh," Jeremy said, his tone saying he didn't understand.

Brace looked thoughtful. "Actually, though we haven't had a lot of contact, I always liked your cousin Donald."

"He avoids family get-togethers. I like him, too, but we haven't talked much in the last few years."

"I think we're off the track. I think we were both thinking it'd be a good idea to let your relatives know we have a family now. That should keep them away."

"Not so. Besides, it wouldn't fend off *your* family for long."

"Then what are you thinking?"

"I'd like to find a bigger place so the children would have more room."

"Good idea."

"It should be on the water. The children love it."

"And have a barn for horses," Jeremy said.

Brace released the trio and moved back. "Let me talk to Jake." He grinned. "This could get interesting."

"We can't move too fast." But she knew Brace could. Once his focus was set, he could make obstacles disappear.

"We were going swimming," Ella said. "Mrs. Duggan was going to take us."

"Destiny and I will take you," Brace said. "Just wait one minute. I need to call Jake."

He crossed the room to make a phone call, his end of it consisting of short bits of speech interspersed with many head nods and shakes. He hung up the phone. "All right. Let's get ready to swim."

Destiny burned to ask him what he'd said to Jake. She was pretty sure the ball was rolling.

They went swimming and stayed in the warm water for quite a time. Ella could now do short strokes on her own. Jeremy splashed a great deal, but he, too, was making progress.

"I wonder if the school has a swim team for their age group," Brace said to Destiny as they sat on the beach watching.

"Be careful, you might be asked to form one."

He grinned. "And I might accept."

When they returned to the condo, Destiny set out snacks while the children changed. Sliced apples, oranges, crackers with peanut butter, and glasses of milk looked inviting. Satisfied, she went to her own room and changed.

By the time she returned to the kitchen, dressed in lightweight pants, a short-sleeved shirt, and slip-ons, the children were already there with Brace. Mouths full, they tried to talk around the food.

"Well? What did Jake say?" Destiny asked Brace while she sipped carrot juice.

"He says there's a big old place not far from The Arbor. It had been in the same family for generations. It's been empty for eight months, ever since the last member of the family, a retired school-teacher, died. Jake has an option on the place he'd be glad to give us, and a work force that could get it ready for us in a matter of days. Can I give him the go-ahead?"

"I'd like to look at it."

He moved closer, studying her tight features. "That's not all that's on your mind."

"I'm still thinking about the incident at the hospital." A week had passed since then, and nothing else had happened. "You know I called some friends in the Bureau and gave them a description of the one man, the driver, and his license plate. I haven't heard back."

"Webb has been investigating. He'll find them."

"They could've been connected to Clyde."

Brace stiffened. "He said he'd get back at you at the hearing. You think he could have hired those guys?"

"I don't know. It's crossed my mind."

He took several deep breaths. "I'll talk to Webb again."

She nodded.

The rest of the afternoon they stayed on the wide terrace overlooking the lake. The children played for a time, then fell asleep on lounges.

"What are you thinking, Destiny?" Brace asked after a long silence.

"How nice it would be to send Clyde to jail for a long stretch."

"With a big, hairy cellmate who's looking for a 'wife.'"

She laughed as he grinned, then he leaned down and kissed her, his mouth lingering.

She edged back, staring at him. "It's—it's soon."

"We're married, Destiny."

She nodded. "I guess I need to get used to that."

He opened his mouth to speak, then shut it again. "I'll accept that."

"Good." They fell silent again, and Destiny drifted off to sleep. She had the sensation of rocking and opened her eyes, staring groggily up at Brace. "Wha . . . What?"

"Jeremy and Ella are pestering me for dinner. Shall I cook again, or would you rather—"

She sat up. "I'll do it."

Dinner was simple. Fresh strawberries with sour cream. Raw carrots and broccoli. Chicken breasts broiled with a mixture of honey and vinegar over brown rice. Milk to drink. Italian ices and fresh ice cream finished the meal.

When Destiny caught Brace grinning at her, she frowned. "What?"

"That was a most interesting meal. Been poring over the *Road to Health* cookbook?"

Chin up, she tried not to smile. "Yes. They need all the nutrition I can fire into them."

"I wondered why you bought the ice cream maker."

"Handy little tool when I want to give them nutrition the easy way."

"Ice cream with chopped nuts and bananas has my vote."

"I thought it might. You've got a sweet tooth."

"Yeah," he drawled, his gaze going over her.

Burned to the backbone, she bolted out of her chair and began to clear the table.

After he'd settled the children with a board game, Brace joined her in the kitchen.

"You've got a pensive look on your face," he said as he helped her load the dishwasher. "What's up?"

"I've been thinking about the house Jake mentioned to you."

"Want to look at it? You could call Mrs. Duggan to watch the kids and we could go."

Too quick, she told herself. *Don't be steamrolled.*

"All right, I'll call her." Destiny went to the phone before she could change her mind.

In less than ten minutes, Mrs. Duggan was there.

"Thanks for coming," Destiny said. "We want to take a look at a house—"

"Hackett's place." Mrs. Duggan nodded. "Been

empty for a time. Not a bad structure. My great-grandfather was one of the workers on it. Hanted, they say."

"Hanted?"

"Got them spirits that come up on you, quick as a bite."

"Oh. Hanted. I understand. We thought we'd look—"

"Thinking to buy it. Heard that."

"You did?" Destiny was taken aback.

"Yep. My cousin Tullamora told me. She's named after an Irish whiskey, don't ya' know."

"I didn't," Destiny said faintly.

"Well, she is. She's a telephone person. Likes to listen on the phone. She heard it from Dorothy Lally's second cousin once removed, Emma—"

"I get the drift."

"Thought you might. You look half smart."

"Thanks." Destiny was so diverted, she felt glued to the floor.

"No need to worry about the young ones, either. Darnell's outside, and so are those new guys the mister hired. Besides, if Clyde tries anything with me, he'll be singing soprano in the choir come Sunday. Not that he ever goes to church."

"I see. Then I won't worry."

"Don't. I got all my cousins watching him too."

"And how many would that be?" Destiny whispered, fascinated.

"Seventy, eighty. Who knows? Related to most folks in these parts. I'm sure you understand."

"I do? Oh. Yes, certainly."

"So you go with the mister, and we'll be right and tight."

"Thank you."

"Don't mention it."

Dazed, Destiny went out onto the terrace, where the children had again fallen asleep. "I think they're in good hands," she said to Brace as she took afghans from the settee and covered Jeremy and Ella.

"Oh? You look strange."

"I feel that way . . . but I sure as hell don't feel the children will be threatened."

Before Brace could say more, she sailed by him down the deck steps, around the side of the condo, up the stairs to the parking lot.

"Wait! What's going on?"

Destiny got into his car, barely containing her laughter. "I think Alexander the Great would be jealous of our army."

"Oh?"

"Eufemia Duggan has all her cousins watching Clyde and the children . . . all seventy or eighty of them."

Brace burst out laughing, starting the car at the same time. "Now I really feel fine."

Destiny put her head back on the leather and felt a surge of goodwill. Things hadn't gone sour with Brace's arrival. On the contrary, they'd gotten better, she thought as he steered the car out onto the lake road.

They followed the curving road for about half a

mile before Brace turned onto a wide gravel drive. "Jake says it goes back almost a mile to the house, which overlooks the lake." Thick pines lined the drive, a natural brake for the north and west winds.

"We're really not that far from the condo, or The Arbor."

He steered around an almost ninety-degree turn and then stood on the brakes. "Damn!" He sank back against the seat, turning off the ignition.

They climbed out of the car, staring at the brick facade of the Italianate Victorian mansion. Despite the out-of-control climbers and thickets clinging to it, and the obvious lack of care, the house had style and elegance.

"Jake says it has about fifteen acres, big rooms, wide corridors, five bedrooms."

Destiny blinked. "Maybe it's not as big as The Arbor, but it looks it to me."

They skirted around several overgrown lilac bushes, working their way to the front of the house, which faced the lake.

"What a view!" Destiny breathed. The trees provided a backdrop for the U-shaped plateau where the house sat, giving it a 180-degree vista from the curved veranda. She pointed. "Dynasty told me that's Wells College over there. She said it was founded by the Wells Fargo people."

Brace smiled and took her arm, turning her so they both faced the house. "A grande dame to be sure, isn't she?"

Destiny nodded, loving the house . . . and the feel of his mouth on her ear.

Brace started to say something else, but stopped. They heard the truck at the same time. He pushed Destiny behind him.

Darnell appeared around the corner of the house. "Hi. Miz Duggan said you were here." He looked at the house. "What ya' think?"

Brace released her, but kept her hand in his. "We like it."

"Good. We'll pull out all the stops for you if you decide to buy it," Darnell said, excitement in his voice. "The construction boys know what you did for those kids. We'll use them all on overtime and they'll go for it. You make some choices and we'll get started right away. If we double-time, we could put you in there in a couple of weeks."

"So soon?" Brace grinned his pleasure.

"Yep."

"That's great." He looked at Destiny. "What do you think?"

"I'm amazed." She glanced at Darnell. "Is it all right if we walk through—"

"Do what you want." He took some keys from a jingling key chain. "The house is solid. I've got catalogues on everything you can think of in the truck if you'd like to look at them."

Delight rivered through Destiny. She'd never had a home where the choices would be hers.

"Go in the side door," Darnell told them. "It leads up into the main hall."

They could afford to buy it, Destiny thought. She was running her business from here. Brace would have to do the same if he stayed. "Maybe we could turn one of the bedrooms into a work room."

"No need," Darnell said. "Got a work room and a library, almost as big as at The Arbor."

"It could work for us," Brace said.

She nodded. Along with the bonding she was feeling with him was fright. She'd put her whole self in when they married. If what they had sundered again, she'd be in pieces. She'd loved him so unrestrainedly, it was fearful to think of giving away so much again. There'd be nothing left if she tried and it didn't work. Emptying her heart, mind, and soul could be lethal the second time. She couldn't come back from another free fall to hell.

Brace tightened his hold on her hand, turning toward her, his gaze intent on her face. She was vaguely aware of Darnell walking away. "Thinking about the past?" Brace asked.

"Yes . . . and it hurts."

"It does, and it's hard to put away. We did say we were going to try for Jeremy and Ella."

Her gaze lifted to his. "I don't have to tell you the statistics. You're as aware as I that bringing children into a family that's had problems can do them harm. And you and I were on the brink of divorce. They've had enough chaos in their lives."

Brace inhaled. "I don't look on our marriage as chaotic."

"Oh? Then what did you call it when your sister-in-law locked horns with my aunt on first meeting? It continued almost every time they met. They made the OK Corral look like a Sunday school picnic."

"It won't continue," he promised. "I won't let it."

She nodded. "It will. You can't stop it. Everyone in our families thinks they're right, including you and me." She swallowed. "That's what's so difficult. We're all right to a certain degree. What's lacking is the capacity to give ground, to compromise. If those mental sumo wrestlers decide to come, and chances are they will, it'll be World War III."

"Then we tell them to bug off, get out of our lives, leave us alone."

She shrugged. "Nice on paper."

"It'll work." He put his arm around her and kissed her full on the mouth. "It has to, Des. I've bet my life on it."

SIX

Seven days later it was put to the test. All hell broke loose, though the polite phrase for it was "a family visit."

"Uncle Tyrrell, Aunt Cordelia, Donald, how good of you to come," Destiny managed to say as she opened the door. Her glance touched each one, then the mountain of luggage threatening to fill the condos' parking lot, as a cabbie pulled yet another suitcase out of the trunk of his cab. "I hope you have lodging . . ." Her voice trailed off at her aunt's shocked look.

"Surely you have room for us, Destiny. We're family," Tyrrell Langhorn said in the same brown-sugar tone he used on his sheepdog.

He was her uncle by marriage to her father's younger sister. Though he was her aunt's second husband, and hadn't been married to her that long, he'd been involved in the family business for years. A college classmate of both Destiny's father and Aunt Cordelia's first husband, he'd always been a part of Destiny's life. Mason Wright, Cordelia's first husband and father to her only son, had been killed in the same elevator accident that had killed Porter Smith, Destiny's father. Porter and Mason had been best friends since childhood, even before kindergarten, and had gone to the same schools right through graduate studies. Many had said they were destined to die together as they'd always been together in life.

Tyrrell Langhorn had been there to console Cordelia when she'd suffered the loss of her husband and brother. Two years after the accident he'd married her.

Destiny cleared her throat. "Well, ah, you see—"

Brace's low-slung Jaguar spun into the parking lot behind the condos, effectively blocking the exit of the cabbie who'd brought the relatives. When Brace got out and leaned on the roof of his car, grinning, there were concerted gasps from both Tyrrell and Cordelia.

The driver got out of his cab again. "Hey, Mac, can you move that beauty? Much as I'd like to admire it, I've got a wake this afternoon." Noting Aunt Cordelia's surprise, the cabbie explained. "Double duty. We handle funerals and weddings, as well as ferrying people to where they want to go." He jabbed an index finger at the sign on his door. "Got one for every occasion. Pays the bills." When he smiled, the space where a molar used to be gapped. "Today isn't business. I have to drive my mother and aunt to the wake and I'll drive for the funeral. Family duty."

"That's Bert Snead," Destiny said, not that the explanation would matter. She glanced away from her aunt, who was looking perplexed. "We'll be at the wake too. And the funeral."

"Whatever for?" Cordelia asked.

"The funeral is for a relative of a very nice person, Pepper Lally. Or maybe it's a relative of Dorothy's. I'm not sure."

"I see," her aunt said, her tone saying she didn't see at all.

"What is he doing here?" Uncle Tyrrell asked in stentorian tones, pointing at Brace. He started down the walk toward the parking lot. "He's no longer in our family."

Destiny followed. "Uncle, Brace is staying with me—"

"Surely not! Disgraceful," Cordelia pronounced, following Destiny. "Destiny, you're divorced. Tyrrell is right. He's no longer part of our family." She turned to Brace. "Go away."

Donald trotted along after them, catching up with Destiny. "He should go, unless Destiny wants him to stay. Do you, Des?"

"I—" Destiny began.

"Not on your life," Tyrrell said.

Brace just grinned. "I think you should keep the cab. You'll be staying down the road at Blessing Hill. Nice condos. You'll be comfortable." He paused. "If you let the cab go, you'll be walking, carrying your luggage."

"How dare you?" Tyrrell demanded in his lowest bass tone.

"Easily," Brace replied.

"Destiny! Speak to that man. He's being insulting."

"No he isn't, Aunt. He's more or less telling you I don't have room for you."

"Damn," Bert muttered. "Why didn't they say Blessing Hill in the first place? I can't miss this wake. It's my uncle, once removed or twice, or something." He shook his head in solemn wonder. "Fell off a bar stool and broke his neck. Wasn't a sterling citizen, but he's kin. Have to do my part."

"I'm not leaving here with that man," Cordelia said.

"It's up to you," Brace said, hunching one shoulder. "You can walk. It's about a mile that way. Maybe your son can carry the heaviest bags."

"I'm in pretty good shape," Donald said, a smile lurking, "but Mother's brought everything except her rosewood desk, and I won't court a hernia. Cabbie, wait for me. I'm going to Blessing Hill, wherever that is. I'm not walking."

"Then get moving. I've got a schedule." Bert glanced at his Mickey Mouse watch and groaned. "My mother will drive a pitchfork through me if I come in when it's over."

Tyrrell muttered. Cordelia moaned. Donald

moved, carrying his two small bags with him to the taxi.

Brace prodded. "You'll be glad for this wonderfully clean air when you start pumping up those hills to your place, Tyrrell. Helluva climb."

"Destiny, I deplore these high-handed ways," Tyrrell said, dragging at his cases. "I don't know how he wormed his way into your life again. I shall call you and make an appointment. Your aunt and I need to talk some sense into you."

"Damned if I understand people," Bert muttered. "Go here, go there. They don't know where the hell they're going." He threw the last big satchel into his capacious trunk. "All aboard, everybody. I'm in a hurry."

There was no time for further conversation. Brace moved his car, parking in his usual slot. Destiny's relatives scrambled into the cab. Bert slammed the door and drove off, his wheels kicking up stones.

Destiny stared at Brace. "What's going on? How did you do that? How did you know they were here?"

"So many questions." He ambled toward her. "The most fun will be tomorrow evening. Blessing Hill is having its annual barbecue. Big affair. Dress jeans, the whole bit. Everyone will be there, together."

"Why does that sound ominous?"

"I don't know. My family will be there too. Did I mention that? Do you think it presents a problem?"

She gaped at him. "Problem? We'll need the National Guard."

He shrugged. "I don't care. The kids will remain here. Webb's people will be watching them."

"And I suppose one of them told you about my family's arrival?"

"Right. Very perceptive of you. I do love those cellular phones." He reached her side, lifted her hand, and kissed the palm, rubbing the third finger. "No ring."

She shook her head. "Both are in a safe-deposit box in San Francisco. I was going to have my uncle send them to you."

"Don't!"

She heard the anger in his voice. "I won't, but I won't be wearing them, since there's no one to reclaim them from the box and . . ." She faltered when she saw him pull a jeweler's box from his jeans pocket. "How did you get them?"

"I didn't. These are different. I inherited them from my grandmother's estate."

Destiny sighed, feeling a tug of sadness. She'd been at the funeral not long before she received the pictures proving Brace's infidelity. "It's hard to imagine a world without Maud."

He nodded.

"I liked her. No, I loved her. She was so real."

"She thought the same about you." He cupped her elbow in his free hand, turning her toward the narrow walk that led to her door. "I have another bargain for you."

"Oh?"

He laughed. "Such a suspicious tone."

"Can you blame me? You've probably orches-
trated the largest bloodbath ever seen in Yokapa
County for tomorrow evening and you offer a bargain?"

"I do."

"All right. Let's hear it." She preceded him in the
door. "Jeremy and Ella will be a little late getting
home. Pepper and Dorothy took them to the store to
buy them some duds." Her smile flashed. "I gave
them my credit card and told them to go crazy. I had
to talk Dorothy out of her cash-only ideas, and that
she needed to go to the discount places. She's a
natural-born bargain hunter." She inclined her head.
"Speaking of bargains, you were saying . . . ?"

He stepped behind her into the kitchen area.
"Now, as I see it, we'll be moving into the new house
in short order. The contractors have been at the
place like a bunch of worker bees. It looks great."
When she didn't respond, simply watched him as a
trapped mouse would eye a cat, he continued. "I was
just there. That's where I got the message you'd been
invaded by Martians."

"My family."

"Same thing."

"Go on."

"I figure once we start moving everything, getting the house in order, we won't have time for rec-
reation."

"I buy that."

"Still cautious?"

"Of course. Continue."

"Since we'll be too busy at first even to take the kids on an outing, we should use every opportunity we have to enjoy ourselves."

"Meaning tomorrow night."

"You're quick, Destiny. I've always said you had a razor-sharp mind."

"Flattering. You were saying . . ."

"Well, if we won't have time for fun later, and if we want to enjoy ourselves tomorrow, we should present some sort of united front."

"I think I see where this is going."

He held out the ring box. "Look at these. She wanted you to have them. She loved you, Destiny. You know that. So do I."

There were no protests she could make. She'd loved his grandmother, who'd been the soul of generosity and kindness with a rapier wit and rock-hard common sense. She took the box and opened it. "My goodness. I've never seen anything like them." Perplexed, she looked up at Brace. "I never saw her wear these." She stared again at the exquisitely wrought wedding ring and ruby engagement ring.

"She didn't after my grandfather died. She took them off and put them away. She wouldn't give them to my father. Said she'd know where they belonged when the time came. I have the letter in my desk at home where she states it has to be you."

"You—you wouldn't lie about this. I know you

wouldn't." Tears filled her throat. She shook her head.

"I wouldn't lie," he whispered.

"How can I wear them? Your family will screech."

"So? That's where the fun comes in, Des. Do they dictate our lives? We have children now. Responsibilities that transcend family squabbles. Let them rave. We'll sit back and enjoy it. What do you say?"

She looked up at him, swiping at her eyes. "It sounds like a reception given by the Marquis de Sade."

"So what? We haven't got the time for their pettiness. Jeremy and Ella are paramount. Aren't they?"

She nodded, surrendering, not just because he was right, but because the rings had belonged to Maud and she'd wanted Destiny to wear them. "They might not fit."

"Try them." Brace removed the wedding ring from the old-fashioned velvet box and slipped it on her finger. "Perfect."

Shaken, Destiny stared at the wrought rose-gold band with hearts and ribbons scrolled on it. "Most rings lose their markings after so many years of wear," she murmured.

"Maud said this one had been made by a master goldsmith in London. It belonged to her husband's grandmother. Very old." He'd moved closer, lifting her hand again. When he slipped the ruby ring on in front of the wedding ring, he hauled in a deep breath. "There."

"Yes." She stared at her finger. When he lifted her hand to his mouth and kissed the rings, a sob caught in her throat. Not since their first meeting had she been so moved, so enthralled, so caught in the lost aura. "This could be dangerous for us." She looked up at him.

He gazed into her eyes. "It could be lethal if we don't try. Look at how much we have to gain, and nothing to lose—"

"Not true."

"—by having a good time."

She blinked, her lips parting. He leaned down and kissed her. He could always read her mind, she thought. It was no surprise to feel the surge of passion, heat, and rightness that went with his touch, and the acceptance that no other man would ever make her respond as Brace could. It would've been more of a surprise had the feelings not come.

When he lifted his head, she drew in a deep breath to steady herself. "What next?" she asked.

His smile was slow, sensual, and very readable. "Well, if it's what I want, we go to bed. What's your choice?"

Blood cascaded through her, suffusing her with laughter, desire, humor, need. All that she wanted in her life! He could give it all to her, he always could. Fear stirred deep within her. How could she part with him a second time if it came to that?

"What?" he asked.

Exhaling, she stared at him. "I was thinking that if we separated after this, it could hurt."

"How about being sundered down the middle and from side to side with a dull saber?"

"Ouch."

"Right. So we'd suffer. We know that and we can put it on a shelf. Neither of us wants to handle it now, if ever." He glanced at his watch. "We don't have much time before dinner. Would you like to see that furniture we ordered from Stickley's? It was just being delivered when I left."

She nodded. So he wasn't going to push that they go to bed, she mused. It wouldn't have taken much persuasion. Used to burying her deeply felt emotions, she let the excitement of being with him, sharing a moment, even such an ordinary one as this, rise to the top of her mind. "I can't believe they were able to get us what we wanted so quickly."

"It's supposed to be some of the best woodworking in the world. I bet it's going to look great in that vintage house." He grinned. "The orientals might be there already too."

"I don't think anyone's ever bought an old house and had it renovated and furnished in such a short time. I feel like we've been on a roller coaster."

"We have. We started our family in a most unconventional fashion."

She laughed. "Yes, but I wouldn't trade Jeremy and Ella for the world."

"Neither would I, and we have some of the best

legal minds in the country seeing to it that we don't lose them."

She shook her head as she walked beside him to the Jaguar. "You're still arrogant in many ways."

"I'm working on it."

She grinned as she seated herself beside him. "I think you are. I also think it's quite an uphill climb." When he winced, she chuckled. "I can't believe I said that."

He sent her a wry look. "I can't say I particularly liked hearing it, but it's got to be healthy for us to air the things we used to cover up."

She nodded. "I promised myself when I moved here that I wouldn't do that anymore."

He was about to start the car, then he turned to her. "I can't help it, Destiny. You're beautiful." He all but lifted her across the console and kissed her over and over again. It was a while before they finally made it to the house.

SEVEN

The next day Destiny and Brace moved. With the help of the two children it turned into a wild misadventure. The upside, Destiny kept telling herself, was that it was a great way for her and Brace to avoid their families.

"I like it here," Jeremy said that night, a ring of orange juice on his mouth as he gazed around the cavernous kitchen. "That's a big 'frigerator, isn't it?"

Destiny nodded, wiping his mouth. "It is. We decided to get the biggest we could find because you like to eat so much."

He nodded. "I do." He yawned, then looked surprised. "It can't be bedtime."

"It is. C'mon. Your sister's already asleep. You need to take a quick bath, then it's off to bed."

"I won't sleep," he said on another yawn.

"Yeah, right."

Destiny was fascinated with the two of them, how

much they'd taught her in such a short time. It was very easy to picture herself as their parent, watching them go off to high school, to college.

"Let's go, young man."

"Destiny, I can undress and wash myself. I don't think you should go in the bathroom with me."

That stopped her. "Uhh, okay. But you have to leave the door open so I can hear you. And you have to wash your hair." His pitying look didn't sway her. "Those are the rules."

He nodded.

Once he was in the bath, his singing and shouting made Destiny laugh as she picked up his soiled clothing.

"He's definitely a basso profundo," Brace said at her back, handing her an errant sock.

"Surely a baritone," she told him. "He's worn out and won't admit it." She nodded toward the bathroom. "He more or less told me he was too big to get undressed in front of me."

Brace grinned. "A man to be sure, though I'd be more than willing to undress in front of you."

"Eager, aren't you?"

"Very." He looked hopeful.

She opened her mouth to tell him to go ahead, when Jeremy shouted to her. "I want you to know I can dry myself."

"Did you wash your hair?"

"Awww."

Brace headed for the bathroom. "I'll be the cop." Destiny chuckled, then went to look in on Ella.

Entranced, she stared at the child's open mouth, the low breaths that seemed to come after at least three heartbeats, the wonderful curling lashes fanned on her cheeks, the flaccid arms that had held Cubby the bear and Shorty the stuffed dog as she'd fallen asleep. "You've won my heart, sweetie. God knows what you'll do to the boys when you're a teenager."

"Not a thing," Brace said from behind her. "She's going into a nunnery. And Jeremy's in bed waiting for his story."

"Oh? Does Ella know she's joining a convent?"

"I have years to convince her. I can be very persuasive."

"What if she wants to marry and have a family?"

"Fine. Thirty-five is a good age to marry."

"Oh Lord, you sound like my great-grandmother who thought women were too young to marry before thirty."

"A very perceptive woman. No girl of mine will marry any younger."

"Might I remind you that I was younger than that when we married."

"You think I don't recall that lustful, rapacious man who went after you hammer and tongs in Hawaii?"

"I'm sure you do."

"I do," he said, his smile fading. "I can't forget."

"Neither can I."

Jeremy's yell broke the spell. They both turned away at the same time, bumping gently.

"Is this what my sister-in-law refers to as the 'sex interruptions' called children?" he said.

Destiny laughed.

By the time they'd seen to Jeremy and he was dozing and yawning, still proclaiming he wasn't tired, Destiny was feeling the need to kick back. "I think I'll shower and go to bed."

Brace stared at her, opened his mouth, closed it, then nodded.

An hour later she'd showered and was in her own bedroom trying to watch television. She gave it up and paced the room. On an impulse she went down the wide staircase to the first floor, easing around groups of unopened cartons in the main hall, making her way to the library. The entire room had been scoured, all the old wood sanded and refinished, and the books that had been left there returned to the shelves. It was an awesome room, and she looked forward to spending time in it. But that night none of the books held her interest.

She climbed the stairs again and was about to open her bedroom door when she saw the shaft of light under Brace's door. Common sense said let it alone, don't bother. Starved sexual responses urged, why not.

She gave in without a whimper.

Her satin slippers gave her a silent approach. Her satin pajamas with the long jacket made a slight whisper as she pushed open his door. He was sitting on the bed, half-glasses on his nose, reports strewn around him, dressed only in silk boxer shorts. Hadn't she given him those? She'd loved choosing his underwear when they'd been together. She recalled how he'd once ordered his suits in bunches. After they married, he'd happily trailed after her through endless stores while she told him what she loved seeing on him. He'd always worn her choices, day and evening.

She wasn't sure what to say, and finally settled on just "Hi."

He looked up and whipped off the glasses, tossing them on the bed. "Are you all right? The children?"

"Everything's fine." She had no idea how to approach the subject, so she decided to be blunt. "I was wondering if you were interested in a little tumble."

He sat forward. "I hope you don't mean parallel bars, mats, or the balance beam."

She could feel her body respond to his husky tone, her nipples hardening, a want rising to flood her. "We don't have a workout room in the house." She coughed to clear the hoarseness from her throat.

"We can make one. Would you like me to come and get you, or would you like to come here?"

"I haven't taken my plan that far yet."

He hopped off the bed, scattering papers and glasses with one clean sweep. "Then let me make that decision. I intend to do my damnedest to see that you stay."

"I'm pretty committed," she said, looking up at him. His crooked smile was very sexy. "I realize that this jump could go either way. That's why I'd like to set some ground rules.

"For making love?"

"Let's call it sex for now."

He shrugged, then bent down and swept her up into his arms, kicking the door shut. "Call it what you will, I think it's great." He strode to the bed and set her on her feet next to it, then whipped back the coverlet. "If we're going to talk, we might as well be cozy."

"Very cute." She smiled because she couldn't help it. Climbing onto the bed, she glanced at a sheet of paper. "Shouldn't you pick up your reports?"

"I'll do it tomorrow." He kicked at the last paper as he slid next to her. "You said ground rules?"

She nodded. "No recriminations if this doesn't work for us. We have to be clinical about it. We enjoy sex and we should have it—"

"I concur," he said in a throaty voice. He kissed her ear.

"I'm serious." She looked at him. "We were pretty sure we could take on the world the first time. And the world got us, two out of three falls."

He stared into her eyes, then lifted her hand to his mouth, kissing each finger, lingering on the wedding ring and ruby. "All right. Ground rules."

"Number one. We don't try to tangle each other up."

"I might have trouble with that, but I'll go along. Go on."

"That if we can adopt the children—"

"And I think we can."

"—we don't let that color our lives."

"I think we should stay together if we have the children."

She inhaled. "What if . . . if you want out, if you find someone else."

"I won't."

"Let's keep it open."

"All right. Anything else?"

She shook her head. "I'm sure there are other things, but I can't think of any."

"Good. Is it all right if I kiss you?"

"Please." She turned her head, catching his mouth, loving the gentle strength. Her heart slammed into her chest at the well-remembered passion built rapidly. "Brace . . ."

"Ummm?"

"Nothing. Doesn't it seem unbelievable?"

"No. I've dreamed of this many times."

"Umm. Maybe that's why you're good at it."

He smiled against her mouth. "Bet on it."

"A hundred bucks says you're not better, but the same."

"Easy money for me."

"Oh? We'll see." She wrapped her arms around his neck.

Their bodies fit as though they'd never been apart, sliding down on the silky sheets, pressing together, needing to find the wonder.

His hand slipped up her side, curving under her breast, closing over the fullness.

His breath sighing into her mouth had the hotness raging through her.

"I love you and I don't give a damn if it doesn't fit the ground rules," he muttered.

"I'm not going to say it," she told him, her grip tightening. "I might not be able to let you go then."

"Feel free to put chains on me," he mumbled into her neck.

"Now?"

"Later."

They held the kiss while he removed her silky sleepwear.

"You always look so sexy in pajamas. How is that?" he asked as he peeled the top from her.

"It's a genetic thing."

He chuckled, blowing soft air over her. "Yeah." His shorts sailed across the room. Then there was nothing between them except soft, panting breaths. He embraced her, his mouth exploring hers, searching as though he had a map. "I'll never get enough."

"Bragger."

"Yeah." He'd covered them with a sheet. Now he lifted it to study her, a half smile on his lips. "You're so beautiful. How do you maintain this wonderful body?"

"I do a great deal of running."

From him! The phrase sang between them, but it died before it could be spoken. Now was not the time.

He slid down her, mouth and hands trailing across her skin. He kissed her thighs. "I've missed this so much."

Destiny thought she'd exploded. When she

opened her eyes, she was sure she'd be in pieces. How could one man's words be more sexy than anything about any other man alive?

She didn't even know she'd taken hold of his head, sending a message, until he looked up at her, eyes dark with passion, his hair tousled. "What?" she asked, not releasing him.

"It's a fantasy, having you hold me again after such a long separation."

"Mere weeks." It had seemed endless to her.

"An eternity."

"Tell me more about your fantasy." She moved her body in sinuous delight over the satiny sheets.

"This is it, our being together again."

She looked at him, taking in the wonder of his virile nudity, the power and grace of his body, the flat belly, the hard sinewed chest and shoulders, his legs and arms long and strong. She knew he worked out, could almost recite his schedule. It didn't dim the joy of looking at him, drinking in the appeal of his masculinity.

He moved up beside her, leaning down to take one of her nipples into his mouth. "I love your body."

She'd always been sure of that, never doubting they had the best sex in the world, that he'd ruined her for any other man.

Lifting his head, he studied the pebble-hard nipple he'd been suckling. "Too perfect."

"Naw," she muttered, entranced with the heat

flooding her, the overwhelming need to love him as much as she could.

He bent his head again, closing his mouth over her once more, sucking and pulling until she whimpered and he was making excited sounds in his throat.

Electricity jolted through her, arching her body, pulling a long moan from her throat, closing her hands around him.

Nothing stopped him. He moved from one breast to the other, pulling her upward so he could have more of her. He was totally carnal in his approach, letting her see and feel his hunger, holding nothing back.

His fingers ran over her legs and stomach as though she were a rare Guarnerius and he a maestro.

Every move he made excited her more.

Destiny heard the sounds, knew she and Brace had made them. There were words, undecipherable, in a lover's tongue that couldn't be translated. She loved the murmurs and the touches. It was her world. She'd needed it and missed it so much.

He levered himself over her. Placing a hand behind each of her knees, he parted them.

Destiny knew by the glow in his eyes what he was going to do. Too soon, too soon, she cried in her heart.

"No, love, it's right."

She might've been stunned that he seemed to read her thoughts, except that he'd always done that.

When he lowered his head, placing his open mouth over her mound, she forgot everything.

Like a skylark she soared, the song deep inside a husky groan caught in her throat. In seconds she climaxed, thinking even as she did, it couldn't happen.

When he entered her, she wanted it more than she ever had. Eager to hold him, she lifted her hips to ease his entry.

He didn't plunge into her as she felt he must. Instead he eased into her in small, shallow thrusts that had her mouth drying, her body trying to close over him, to keep him with her. As he quickened the pace, her blood and spirit built again into the passion, until their lovemaking was wilder than a hurricane, more wonderful than the first love they'd shared.

When he put his hand between them and touched her, she felt crazed with want. The tempo increased, bringing her to an exquisite brink once more. Out of breath, trying to call out to him not to stop, never to cease, caught in the maelstrom of beauty that few achieve in physical love, she clung to him, whispering his name in her soul.

When he came, she was already in the throes of her second orgasm, stunned by the force that seemed to hurl her into space, revealing to her the panorama of love that had changed her life once and now put her through a new metamorphosis.

Charged, changed, energized, and more at peace than she'd ever been, she wanted to laugh out loud at the pure joy of such a coupling. Knowing each other as they did, they'd pushed to an even greater plateau. Their senses had sizzled with the power of their coming together.

As she was replete in body, so was her mind.

Caught in his own euphoric aftermath, he lifted her hand with the new rings on her finger and kissed them.

Feeling giddy with a happiness she hadn't expected, she turned and pressed her mouth against his ear. "Was it as good for you as it was for me?"

Laughing, he caught her in his arms. "Better and you know it. You owe me big time."

"That's your ego talking."

He shook his head. "How good was it, Des?"

"Umm, not bad."

"Not bad?" He caught her under the arms, lifting her so he could suckle on her breast again. "It was perfect."

The huskiness in his tone drove her crazy. In seconds she was clutching him, and the dance of angels began once more. She did owe him. How much was the bet? Had they said a hundred? It should have been a million.

EIGHT

"Yes, Mother, I heard you," Brace said, rolling his eyes at Destiny while continuing his phone conversation. "I don't see how Destiny and I could've stopped it." Long pauses followed, with Brace alternately nodding, grimacing, and biting back laughter.

When he hung up and leaned back in his chair, Destiny waited for about three seconds before bursting out, "Well? What's going on?"

"All hell's broken loose. You know how your cousin Donald and my sister Bel have been hanging out together so much since the families arrived last week?"

Destiny nodded cautiously.

"Well, it seems the two of them got, shall we say, very friendly last evening."

"That shouldn't be a concern. Donald's engaged to some woman named Kimberley Marchese. They met at Smith-O'Malley, Uncle Tyrrell said."

"What's she like?" Brace asked.

"You're grinning like a Cheshire cat. Why?"

"Tell me about Kimberley Marchese."

Destiny shook her head. "I really don't know her. Uncle Tyrrell hired her a few months before I moved out here. I'm sure your mother has nothing to worry about. Isn't Bel involved with someone?"

"I thought so."

"What does that mean?"

"It seems Bel and Donald have eloped."

"What?" Openmouthed, Destiny sat forward. "I don't believe it. Both are tied to other people. There must be some mistake."

"Apparently not."

Destiny bit her lip. "The last conversation I had with Donald, right before I moved here, was about the monthly stipend the company's been sending him. He said he didn't need the money. I suggested he donate some of it to charity, and also that he let us hang some of his paintings in the company atrium." She paused, thinking.

"What?" Brace asked.

"I'm certain he never mentioned a fiancée to me then, but that doesn't mean anything. He's never been particularly talkative. Still, it's bizarre."

"It's a riot," Brace said, not able to contain his mirth. "My mother sounded like she was biting through steel."

Destiny shook her head. "Bel and Donald. I wish them well."

When he laughed again, she gave him a look of

warning. "You may think it's funny now. The flip side, though, is no one will leave the county until this is sorted out." It was her turn to laugh when his face fell and he looked pained.

"That's not humorous," he said, throwing himself into a chair. A pensive expression on his face, he stared at her.

"What?"

"Are you happy we took this house? Can you live through the rest of the renovations?"

"Yes," she answered slowly. She was sure he had something else on his mind. "I'm pleased at how fast the work has gone, how sturdy the foundation is," she continued.

He looked out the window of the library. It faced the lake, as did most of the main rooms of the place. "I like everything about this house."

"So do I."

He faced her again. "Do you think you can ever believe that I was faithful to you, Destiny?"

"That came from left field," she whispered.

"Yes. Can you?"

"Yes."

He shot forward in his chair, his hands reaching for hers, then retreating before he touched her. "Please believe in me. I want that so much." He got out of his chair and knelt in front of her, kissing her. With his mouth on hers, he spoke. "Bel always said I had the hots for you. She's right."

Destiny laughed, her heart pounding.

The phone rang. Brace cursed. Destiny picked up

the receiver. "Yes, I heard, Uncle Tyrrell. I'm sure Aunt Cordelia will be able to handle it. Yes, I'm sure she's very upset. Please don't worry. Of course. See you then." She replaced the receiver. Brace was back in his chair, his brooding gaze on her. The wonderful moment of near understanding had dissipated.

"You're annoyed," she said softly.

"I'm just wondering when we'll get on with our lives. My office will soon be set up on the second floor of the barn." He glared at her. "Everything would be in place if we didn't have an interfering family."

"So I guess now is not the time to tell you that my family and yours are coming here to dinner this evening. And you can bet it won't be for the food. My guess is, as far as my aunt and uncle go, they'll want to map out a strategy to break up Bel and Donald."

"What? You really think they'd try that?" He shook his head.

"Yes . . . maybe . . . I don't know." She sighed. "My aunt and uncle are not happy about this. I got the impression from Tyrrell that both he and my aunt thought this Marchese woman was perfect for Donald. I guarantee there will be some sort of brouhaha about the elopement."

"Bull. It's not their business."

"I don't think they will see it that way. You've admitted your mother is upset."

"To hell with the lot of them. I'm not going to—"

The phone rang, interrupting him. Before Destiny could reach for it, he scooped it up and barked a greeting. His expression softened almost immediately. "Bel? Is it you?" He punched a button to activate the speaker phone.

"Yes. Are they going to eat us alive?"

"Probably," Brace answered.

Destiny made a face at him. "Are you all right, Bel?"

"I've never been so right in my life. You know Donald and I are married."

"Yes."

"I'm very happy."

"Good," Brace and Destiny said at the same time.

"Donald's right here."

"Congratulations," Destiny said.

Donald chuckled. "Thanks. I'm as happy as Bel. I'll face the music when we return, but we're going somewhere to be alone first, then we'll handle that."

"Go to Waikiki," Brace said. "You know where my place is, Bel. I'll call Sturdevant and he'll have it ready for you." Brace glanced at Destiny, who stared back, memories crowding them.

Brace smiled. "What do you say?"

"Wonderful! We might never come home," Bel chortled.

"That might be the smart move," Destiny said. "Your parents and my relatives are gathering here this evening, no doubt to plan a strategy."

"Ugh!" Bel's disgust came through the phone.

"What sort of strategy?" Donald asked, suspicion in every syllable.

"I think you've guessed," Brace said before Destiny could answer. "They'd like to sink your boat."

"Not a chance," Donald said.

"Good. Stay out in Hawaii for a few weeks," Brace suggested. "Do some surfing and all that tourist stuff."

"Or we could be like you and Destiny and never leave the bedroom for three weeks."

"Bel!"

Destiny winced at Donald's laughing remonstrance.

Brace shouted with laughter. "Right. Go for it."

"We will. There won't be a better time," Bel said. "Maybe I'll come back pregnant."

"Put a sock in it, Bel," her new husband suggested.

Destiny was still chuckling when they hung up the phone.

Brace leaned close to her. "All my sister's bragging has gotten my active mind picturing things. Let's go upstairs and I'll act out my fantasies."

Destiny should have said they couldn't, that their guests would be arriving within hours, that Jeremy and Ella would be returning soon. "All right."

Brace blinked, swallowed, then beamed. Within seconds he was scooping her up, laughing, and running.

He almost made it across the center hall to the stairs.

The front door bell rang.

He glared at the door. "It can't be anyone important. No members of our families are polite enough to ring a bell, and no one else is worth the trouble."

"Put me down. I have to answer."

"No."

"Yes. Another time." She smiled at him, even though her insides were churning with frustration.

Brace let her slide down his body. "I'm personally going to punch anyone who's at the door."

"You can't." She wiggled back from him and went to the door as the bell chimed again. Opening it, she stared at a delivery man dressed in a brown uniform and cap. "Yes?"

"Miss Smith? Sign here."

Destiny did, took the package, and shut the door. "Oh. It's from Smith-O'Malley. Maybe some office supplies. I mentioned to my assistant that I needed some, but I intended to purchase them here." She reached for the side of the package to tug it open when Brace took it from her hands.

"Sorry, this goes in the kitchen. Wait here."

He was back in seconds. Destiny grinned at him when he gathered her into his arms again.

They made it to the top of the stairs before someone slammed the front door and called out.

"No," Brace groaned. "Is that who I think it is?"

"Jeremy."

The door slammed again. Another voice chimed

in, calling to them. Then the door slammed a third time.

"This is bad," Brace muttered, letting Destiny stand.

"Parents would call it normal." When he groaned again, she bit her lip.

"Go ahead, laugh. You have no heart."

She did then, peal after peal as she descended the stairs.

Ella and Jeremy appeared, grinning, telltale circles of ice cream around their mouths. "Hi," they said together.

"Hi, yourself. I guess I should have gone with you. I didn't get any ice cream."

"I didn't get what I wanted, either," Brace said at her back.

Mrs. Duggan appeared from the kitchen. "What should I do with that box? I don't want it on my table."

"Oh, put it anywhere. It's probably paper for the printer or some such thing."

"Fine. I'll put it in the storage shed next to the barn. You can keep your necessaries there. Better there than on my table," she muttered, walking back down the hall.

"Right you are, Mrs. Duggan," Destiny said, fighting an irresistible urge to laugh and beg forgiveness at the same time. "Uh, by the way, Mrs. Duggan . . ."

The older woman stopped and turned, and Destiny explained about the unexpected company for dinner, adding that if Mrs. Duggan thought it best, they could contact a catering service about handling the meal.

"Huh!" Mrs. Duggan responded. "As if you could get one of those fancy caterers on such short notice. I'll take care of the cooking. You figure out what you want to serve and I'll call up some of my nieces and have them come over to help. Now, I'll have to get to the kitchen and start things." Mrs. D eyed them up the stairs. "I won't take no back talk in my kitchen."

"Of course not," Destiny answered, wondering if that was the right response.

"I always set my cards on the table."

"Yes. Good idea."

"Pushover," Brace whispered into her ear.

She lightly jabbed her elbow into his ribs. When the housekeeper disappeared to the back of the house, she looked over her shoulder. "You're not much better. Why didn't you tell her to buzz off?"

"I'm too much of a gentleman."

"And she scares the pants off you."

"That too."

The evening began in a funereal way that would have done credit to a monarch's demise.

Drinks were taken with a sigh or a crocodile smile. Eyes were rolled while assorted canapés were popped into mouths. Greetings were given on wisps of air escaping from constricted throats.

"How—how are you, Aunt Cordelia?" Destiny managed to say as Brace went through contorted actions at her relative's back. He sliced his hand across his throat, rolled back his eyes, and staggered.

"Have a pig in a blanket?" Mrs. Duggan thrust the plate between the two women. "Bound to take the edge off your miseries. Think how bad the pig feels about being your enjoyment and it'll perk you right up." She grabbed one and all but plunged it into Aunt Cordelia's mouth.

Mouth slack, Destiny waited for the explosion as her aunt chewed, plucked out the toothpick, and swallowed. "Good, aren't they?" Destiny said.

Cordelia blinked. "Amazing. They are quite good." She eyed the tray as Mrs. Duggan moved away. "You might tell her, Destiny, that there's no need to keep up a monologue to cover the dead silence in this room. I'm sure you must have some music you might play."

"Ah, well, you see, we haven't too much furniture or many appliances as yet. We haven't had the time to go shopping for them. So . . . we don't have a stereo."

"Oh dear, that is a shame." Cordelia blinked again, her gaze following the tray around the room, then she sighed. "I commend you for not bringing up the subject of Donald and the family disgrace, dear. It shows remarkable and admirable restraint."

Destiny sucked in air. "Aunt Cordelia, I owe you so much. When I lost my parents, you were there for me. You showed me every consideration, and I thank you for that. But I will not disparage Donald for following his heart."

Cordelia's hand went to her breastbone. She seemed to sway with surprise. "You won't?"

"No."

"Tyrrell says we must, that we need to take every opportunity to encourage Donald to end this foolish marriage. Tyrrell intends to tell him that his job won't be waiting for him unless he does."

Heat and ire made Destiny's stomach boil. Forcing down the bile, she fisted her hands, facing her aunt. "Since I am the chief executive officer of the corporation, I will tell Uncle Tyrrell that will not occur." She struggled to calm herself. "Besides, Donald is devoted to his painting. I think he plans to stay in New York when they return."

"Return? Do you know where they are?"

Destiny almost smiled. Her aunt's vacuity could disappear in an instant when there was something she wanted to ascertain. "Why would they tell me?"

Cordelia relaxed. "True. I'm sure they're closeted in some dingy room in some horrid, germ-ridden hotel."

"Umm." Destiny pictured Brace's home on Oahu, not far from Waikiki Beach. "How unfortunate."

"Yes, it is." Cordelia gestured for Brace to come to her side. "Destiny was just commiserating with me about Donald and your sister."

"She was?" Brace's glance flashed to Destiny, who was expressionless. "Oh. She was. Yes, the whole thing is . . ."

"Shocking?" Destiny offered.

"Yes, that's it."

Tyrrell came up to them, much like an approaching Cape buffalo. "Well, does anyone know where they are? We should get them back as soon as possible."

"Why?" Brace asked.

"Why? My boy, the sooner this mess is scotched, the better. He'll be a long time wishing for his job back when I see him. He's in need of strong words."

"He's also an adult," Brace said mildly. "A man I would be happy to have working for me. That is, if he doesn't pursue another career entirely." Brace seemed not to notice Tyrrell's mottled features as the older man puffed a protest.

Before Tyrrell could speak, Mrs. Duggan sailed back into the room. "Food's on. It'll get cold quick, so get a move on," she told them, then wheeled around and left.

"A rather strange woman," Cordelia exclaimed.

"Deuced pest if you ask me," Tyrrell said. "I thought she was going to ask me for my identification when I came to the door."

"You mustn't mind her. She's protecting the children." Destiny tried to soothe her uncle.

"Humph, that's another thing I don't like. Bringing strangers into the family."

"Every baby's a stranger until you get to know him or her," Brace said, taking Destiny's arm when her eyes flashed and chin jutted. He led her from the room. "We should have let Ella and Jeremy stay up and eat with us. Our guests might've left early."

"My uncle shouldn't have said that." Her chin quivered.

Before Brace could respond, someone touched his arm and he turned. "Mother. Dad. Enjoying yourselves?"

"I must confess that I'm not," Susan Coolidge said. "I'm worried about Bel."

Her husband put his arm around her. "Don't worry, love."

"But, John—"

"Dad's right, Mother. Bel will be fine. Now, we should get to the dining room before Mrs. Duggan comes after us with a broom."

Susan tried to smile when her husband laughed, but it was a poor effort.

Brace continued along with Destiny. "Why don't we send everybody home?" he whispered.

"Shh, your mother and father will hear."

He shook his head. "I don't think so. They're too caught up with Bel and Donald at the moment."

Destiny winced. "I don't feel right about not telling them where Donald and Bel are."

"We can tell them before they leave tonight, if you like."

"I do. I know how I'd feel if I couldn't find my child."

He grinned, putting an arm around her. "You're one tough mama."

"I'm beginning to think I am."

They entered the dining room arm in arm.

Chairs scraped on the hard wood floor; silverware

tinkled as it was lifted. Mrs. Duggan's nieces finished serving and melted into the kitchen.

"I feel for poor Kimberley," Tyrrell said, looking satisfied as he gazed at his plate mounded with food. "She was planning a life with Donald."

"Really? What kind of life?" Brace asked.

Tyrrell looked discomfited. "My boy, surely you know. She wanted a family, and with Donald being heir apparent to a company, she felt secure."

Brace put down his fork, smiling, his tone affable. "Is that a fact? I thought Jeremy would be in line for that."

Destiny tried to get Brace's attention. She coughed, cleared her throat, tapped her fork against her plate.

Cordelia, on her left, leaned toward her. "Really, dear, you must try not to fidget. The men are having a conversation."

Destiny rolled her eyes.

"I think Bel showed balls," Laura, Brace's sister-in-law, said. "How about that? It's poetic. Bel and balls. I like that."

Destiny had been about to sip some wine. She took too much and coughed.

"I don't," John Coolidge said. "But as for Jeremy not being able to take his place in Destiny's company, I wouldn't worry. Surely there's enough room for him in yours, son."

Tyrrell looked purplish again. "We were talking about Donald. And I say again it's not in the boy's best interest if he thinks he can hurt someone the way he's hurt Kimberley. He must be made to toe the line. Letting him understand he could be in line for Destiny's job is one way to do that."

"I don't think so," Brace said.

Tyrrell frowned as though he was about to expound on the subject, but then he seemed to think better of it. "I'm sure the young man Bel was seeing is feeling the same sorrow as Kimberley."

"Don't bet on it," Laura said. "Trent has a wandering eye. Probably has quick hands too."

"Laur, please," her husband Michael, Brace's younger brother, said. "Let's not push our luck."

"Don't worry. He never bothered me. I would've decked him." Laura grinned at her spouse.

"Please," Susan Coolidge said. "Let's not get into a silly argument. I admit I wasn't happy at first about this marriage between Bel and Donald." She held up her hand as Tyrrell started to speak. "What's important is that they're happy. Isn't that right, John?" She turned to her husband.

"Yes, my love, it is." He grinned at her, then winked at Destiny. "And as long as we're on the subject of love—"

"I don't think we were," Tyrrell said.

"—I'm going to propose a toast to my daughter-in-law. I'm happy you've decided to put up with my son. I hope it continues. You were always a favorite of mine."

Destiny was stunned.

"Thanks," Laura said. "I needed to hear that."

"Laur," Michael moaned.

John patted Laura's arm. "You've always been aces with me. That hasn't changed." He smiled when Laura blushed and kissed his cheek.

"Thank you, sir," Destiny said, swallowing. "That's very good of you."

"Not really. I have an ulterior motive. I want those grandchildren, Jeremy and Ella."

"They are sweet, aren't they?" Cordelia said, earning a grimace from her husband.

"They are," Susan concurred. "I don't see why we can't coordinate holidays so that we can all spend time with the children. What do you think, Cordelia?"

"I think that's wonderful, Susan. We could—"

"Nonsense!" Tyrrell exclaimed, spearing a prawn. "Those children aren't even in the family yet. I don't think we should jump fences here."

Destiny rose to her feet, staring down the table at her uncle. "I should tell you that Brace and I want the children, that we mean to have them, and that I intend to spend whatever it takes to secure them in our lives."

"Hear, hear." John applauded.

Brace sat back, chuckling. "Back off, Tyrrell. She's exhibiting all the earmarks of a cornered mama. She might attack."

Destiny sank down in her chair, her smile lopsided. "I just might do that." She was going to say more when Mrs. Duggan walked into the dining room carrying a portable phone. "You can take a message, Mrs. Duggan—"

"I think you'll want to take this one." She plunked the phone down in front of Destiny.

"Excuse me." Destiny glanced around the table, then picked up the phone. "Yes?"

"It's Bel. I figured by this time they would be holding the wake. Donald said they'd be raking you over the coals too. So . . . if you can, put me on a speaker. Donald and I will defend our marriage."

Destiny smiled. "All right." She turned to Mrs. Duggan and asked her to bring in the speaker phone from the library.

The others watched, puzzled. Destiny said nothing. When Mrs. Duggan placed the speaker phone in front of her and plugged it in, Destiny punched the button. "Go ahead. You're on."

"Mother, Dad, it's Bel. I'm fine and very, very happy."

John leaned across the table toward the phone. "Are you all right?"

"I'm wonderful. So is Donald."

The long pause seemed to magnify breathing sounds. Time suspended for seconds.

"Darling . . . are you sure?" her mother asked.

"Yes, Mother. I've never been more sure of anything."

"Mrs. Coolidge, I want to cherish your daughter all our days." Donald's voice was steady and sure.

Brace looked over at Destiny. He smiled when

she reddened, and she knew he remembered. Those words had been part of their wedding vows.

She gave one shake of her head as though that would control him and make him think he'd made a mistake.

He smiled. Wait and see, he seemed to say.

NINE

A few days later Destiny finished her work early and decided to take a walk. She hadn't really had time to explore the property she'd acquired. As she breathed in the fresh air, she thought of how at home she felt there, at peace, with little desire to live elsewhere. Brace's presence cemented that.

Nearing the modernized tool shed behind the house, she paused. Hadn't Mrs. Duggan said she'd put the package she'd received in there? Pushing open the double doors, she was pleased to note the well-built structure was clean and in good order inside as well as outside. She saw the package almost at once. It sat on a shelf under some hanging tools. She decided to open it there. She had just lifted an edge of the brown wrapping paper when she saw a pencil-thin line of smoke.

"Damn!" Destiny whirled, flung open the door,

and ran, trying to get to the shelter of the house. She almost made it.

Boom! Boom!

The blasts slammed her to the ground hard enough to take her breath. Glass shards and shattered boards sailed around her. There was a stinging in her thighs and arms.

Silence.

Then shouts.

Spitting grass and dirt out of her mouth, Destiny didn't move.

"Des! Dammit, Des, are you all right?"

She felt herself lifted, and turned to Brace. "I'm—I'm all right. I saw the smoke and I guess my training kicked in and told me to run."

"Good, good," he crooned, holding her. "I'm getting you to the hospital. You're bleeding."

"No, no. I'm all right. I think I just cut my legs on flying glass." Destiny tried to smile up at him. Still shaken, all she could manage was a grimace. "Let me get in the house. I know I'm not really hurt."

Before she could move, Brace scooped her into his arms, carrying her into the kitchen.

"She all right?" Mrs. Duggan asked, indicating he set Destiny down on the table. "Used to do nursing. Let me take a look." She jerked her head toward the singing kettle. "Put that hot water in the pan. Baking soda's in there." She pointed at a cupboard. "Get the peroxide." She glared down at Destiny. "What happened?"

"The package that was delivered to me, that you put in the shed, started to smoke—"

"What?" Brace turned from the cupboard, his teeth clamped together. "Are you saying this wasn't an accident?"

"Like one of those pipe bomb things. Mercy. This country's going to the dogs." Mrs. Duggan bent over her, prodding and pushing, then wiping the superficial cuts with peroxide. "Seems okay. I'll clean these. You'll live to fight another day."

Brace winced. "I hope her fighting days are over. Could you go over that again?"

Destiny told them what had happened.

Mrs. Duggan shook her head. "I'll call the sheriff. Funny how I just didn't want that package in my kitchen."

"Thank God," Brace murmured, cuddling Destiny.

The back door burst open.

"Mind you don't slam the door, Darnell," Mrs. Duggan admonished. "I have a cake in the oven."

"Yes, ma'am." Darnell closed the door with great care. "What happened?"

"Pipe bomb," Mrs. Duggan said. "Don't spread it around the county. We might have to get the Feds in on this." She grinned at the openmouthed men. "I watch all the cop shows."

Destiny's limbs were stinging, as were her thoughts. Someone had sent her a bomb! Why? Who was her enemy? She'd have to call the Bureau.

What if one of the children had opened that package?

Brace put his arms around her, then turned to Darnell. "Let's talk when I come downstairs. I want to get her into the shower and then to bed."

Destiny was going to argue, but reaction was setting in, as it always did. Her mind and reflexes were quick, her response time excellent. Afterwards she always turned to jelly. "A shower sounds good."

Brace studied her for a moment, then strode from the kitchen, holding her in his arms.

"I'll make the tea, then we'll discuss how we'll protect ourselves," Mrs. Duggan called out.

Destiny heard Darnell's quiet "Yes, ma'am" and she gave a watery chuckle.

Brace carried her straight to the bathroom attached to their master bedroom.

"I'll be out in a minute," she said as he set her down. Actually she wanted to stay in his arms. "I didn't expect that," she added, her hands starting to shake.

"Thank God you've got quick reflexes." He hugged her. "Damn the sons of bitches who are frightening you. Webb needs to know about this."

"The children. They need to be watched. If they'd tried to open . . ." She cleared her throat. "They could've been in so much danger. Do you think Cyde—?"

"That will be checked. You can bet on it." He kissed her cheek. "You were great."

"Jeremy and Ella are vulnerable."

"I know. They'll be fine. So will you. I promise that."

He helped her undress, then stared at her. "Have I told you that I love your body?"

"Yes."

"Well, did you know that if you weren't around, my life would be over? See? I have no choice. I have to keep you alive."

Stunned by his words, she sagged against the wall.

He caught her in his arms, cradling her. "You've had a shock. I'll get in the shower with you."

He stripped off his own clothes, letting them fly in every direction, then turned on the water. After helping her in, he grabbed a loofah sponge and soaped it.

"You needn't wash me. I can do it," she told him even as her hands clutched his waist.

"Like to do it," he responded, kissing her. "My favorite pastime is touching you."

"You're saying I'm a hobby," she murmured, her lips rubbing his.

"The only one I want."

Her hands slid to his bare back, massaging there, bringing him closer. When he gasped, she smiled.

"Temptress," he said.

"Don't hold back," she crooned, undulating her body, loving the feel of the warm water sluicing between them, making them slippery, sexy. Desire was a banked fire that began to flame.

When he cupped her backside and brought her

up against him, he groaned, whispering carnal phrases that had her body burning in response. "I love you. I never stopped."

"I love you too," she whispered in his ear, blasting the last barriers between them, exposing her vulnerability.

A blistering need overtook them, firing away the questions, the uncertainties that had colored their actions and feelings for too long.

So much had to be decided, but she no longer doubted that she loved him.

When she felt him slide her down his body, experienced the silken penetration that caught at her breathing, she smiled, eyes closed, intent on every sensation.

With every thrust, she pushed downward, wrapping her legs around his waist. In a crushing rush she found her climax, stunned at the speed, at the completeness of it. She couldn't find her voice to tell him.

Her swaying, plunging body was all the telegraphing he needed. In concert with hers, his body thrummed to culmination, the volcano catching him, circling him, keeping him.

"Tea's ready," Mrs. Duggan bellowed from the hall outside the bedroom. "And Darnell's still waiting for you, Brace Coolidge. Get a move on."

Destiny collapsed against him, mirth overtaking her. "You'd better hurry."

"That woman will drive me nuts," Brace muttered, then grinned when Destiny went into gales of laughter. He stepped out of the shower and slapped a towel around himself, then leaned back in to kiss her on the breast. "I'll be back."

After he left, Destiny got out of the shower, dried off, and wrapped herself in Brace's voluminous robe. In the bedroom she lay down on the bed, intending to think through what had happened and who could be trying to hurt her. She was asleep within minutes.

When she awoke, the room had darkened and Brace was sitting beside her on the bed. "Darnell gone?" she asked sleepily.

"Yes." He leaned over and kissed her throat.

She sighed, her eyes closing. As quickly as that, she recalled in frightening detail what had happened—the smoke, the explosion, her fear.

Her eyes flashed open. "Hold me, Brace."

He moved swiftly, lying down beside her and pulling her close, her head cradled on his shoulder. She smiled, eyes closing again. She needed his comfort so much.

"Will you marry me, Destiny?"

She lifted her head, her hair falling down over them. "You said we still are married."

"We are. I just want to go through a ceremony with you again. Just you, me, and the children."

A sob rose in her throat. "That's lovely."

"Yeah. I thought we could have a second anniversary thing every year that the kids would celebrate with us. You know, a second birthday for them as our children, and a second chance for us."

She collapsed on his chest. "I want that. I guess I always have. I'm a little afraid, I have to admit."

"It's scary, but we can do it. How many people start out with such a great family?"

"There is the power of numbers." She hesitated. "There's also the danger that could threaten you and the children if someone from my past is out to get me."

"You think someone from one of your cases is on a vengeance kick? You've been out of the FBI for years."

"I know. Still, you can't help but run up against some very nasty people when you're with the Bureau. It's part of the job."

He nodded, his hand stroking her hair. "I swear I'm not going to let you out of my sight from now on." He paused. "You still haven't said you'd marry me."

"Wonderful idea, but . . . I'd like to table it until I know who set those goons after me at the hospital and who ordered the bomb."

His eyes narrowed. "We will find out, I promise you." He curled her under him, leaning over her. "I am not going to lose you again." He kissed her, his mouth slanting over hers, his tongue delving.

In moments they were so hot, they couldn't get close enough, and they soared together to another blazing culmination.

TEN

The courtroom was all but empty. The early September day was mild, not too hot, with a breeze blowing through the open windows, circulating the stale air. Sun filtered through dust motes, painting macabre shadows on the walls as the judge left the room.

Destiny felt stifled, as though she'd held her breath too long and couldn't get air started again.

"It's over. The preliminaries are complete," Divinity said to her. "Except for a few minor legal details, it's a done deal. Jeremy and Ella will be yours in about a year's time. Congratulations, you two. You deserve it."

"I can't believe it," Destiny murmured.

Brace kissed her. "Believe it."

"I have to get back to the office." Divinity kissed Destiny and gave a thumbs-up sign to Brace. Then she was gone.

Brace looked at her. "Shall we go?"

She nodded and rose. When he took her hand, she squeezed his.

"We did it," he said, pulling her into his arms.

"Yes, yes, they're ours."

They held hands, looking at each other.

"It's a beginning," Brace said.

Destiny nodded. "Let me find a rest room. The worry has gotten to me."

He chuckled. "I'll wait for you in the hall." He walked her out of the courtroom and down to the door marked Ladies.

Destiny was washing her hands when she saw the reflection of two people behind her. The mirror had to be badly warped, she thought, because their images were so fuzzy. A man and woman? What was a man doing in there? "Sorry. You're in the wrong place." Even as she spoke, she thought there was something familiar about them.

"I'll be going," the man said. "I wanted to tell you to be careful. The closest to your heart are your enemies."

A light went on in her brain. "You were the two in the water. Weren't you?"

She whirled to face them, but they were gone. "Wait. What did you mean? Hello. Where are you?" She looked all around the room, even pushing open the cubicle doors. No one.

Leaving the bathroom, she spotted Brace leaning against the wall a few yards away. As soon as he saw her, he started toward her.

"What's wrong?" he asked anxiously when he reached her.

"The man and woman who came out of there—"

"What?" He pushed her behind him, then thrust open the ladies' room door. "A man? And a woman?"

"They came out just ahead of me. You must have seen them."

He shook his head, looking up and down the hall. "I didn't see anyone come out of there but you."

"Oh. You must've been looking away when they left."

"Did they bother you? Did they threaten you?"

"They startled me just by being there, but I didn't feel endangered. In fact I . . ." She paused.

"What?"

She moved her shoulders as though what she had to say wasn't credible. "They seemed friendly. They reminded me . . ."

"Of what?"

"The time in the water when those people helped me." She bit her lip. "It was as though they were old acquaintances. They were warning me, I'm pretty sure." She shrugged. "I could be wrong." It still astounded her that she hadn't told them to get lost. Why hadn't she screamed or taken defensive action?

"What did they say?"

"Something about the people closest to me being my enemy."

He grimaced. "Meaning me?"

"I don't know. I didn't think that."

"Did you recognize the man or the woman?"

"I don't think so, though there was something familiar about them."

Brace's features closed into a cold mask. "Describe them."

"I don't know if I can. I was looking at their reflections, and the mirror must have been foggy or something. I just didn't get a clear look at them." She took a deep breath and concentrated. She'd been trained to be observant. "They both were of medium height and build. The man's coloring was light, the woman's darker. Their clothes were nondescript, yet I got the sense that they were old in some way. Sounds crazy, I know."

"Where the hell is Webb? He should be here."

Destiny tried to pat his arm, but he encased her in his embrace. "Don't get uptight, Brace. I wasn't frightened."

"No? Well, I am. And I'm damn well not going to allow you to be threatened, coerced, or intimidated. Clear?"

She bit back a smile. "Perfectly."

He looked down at her. "Sweetheart, I'm a bear. I know it. I just can't let you be hurt."

She leaned against him, closing her eyes for a moment. "I feel safe. I have since you arrived on my doorstep."

"But you've been frightened more than once, right under our noses. It's going to stop."

"Fine with me." She felt calm, but curious. Who

were that man and woman? She had the feeling she should know them.

"Let's get out of here," Brace said. "I want to talk to Webb."

They crossed the courthouse lobby and Brace hustled her out of the building, checking around him, keeping her close.

"I'm fine, you know," she said.

"Great. I intend to keep it that way."

They'd almost reached the car when Webb seemed to appear out of the ground. He was a nondescript man who looked as out of shape as the rumpled suit he wore. Brace had told her he held a black belt in karate and was a crack shot. He looked more like a cherubic grocer. He studied them for several seconds, his body stiffening, his eyes sharpening. "What's up?"

Brace's grin was hard. "Glad to see you." He related what Destiny had told him.

Webb nodded once, then seemed to vanish.

"How does he do that?"

"Practice, Des." He settled her in the passenger seat of his car, then went around and got behind the wheel.

"I'd like to send the children somewhere," Destiny said.

Brace nodded. "Let's talk to Divinity. As I see it, Jeremy and Ella are in our care. We're their guardians, according to the judge's decision. We'll be their full-time parents in a year. If we think they'd be safer with Mike and Laura, let's say, I think there could be a precedent for that. Check it out with Divinity."

"I will."

In a week it was settled. The children flew off to Colorado with Mike, Laura, and their children. Destiny missed them. She felt disoriented and out of sync without them, but she could live with that. Knowing they were safe mitigated the lost feeling.

There'd been a few tears from both children when it was time to leave, but neither one had suffered trepidation. Destiny had feared they might. She had held back her own grief at parting from them until they left, then she'd buried her face in Brace's neck and sobbed.

"They'll be back, sweetheart," he'd said, "and for now they're safe."

"I know." Destiny missed them, but there was tremendous relief knowing that.

Now she needed to look at her life, into her past, for some clues about who was threatening her. She'd talked to the Bureau and gotten the names of three particularly nasty people she'd helped put away who were now back on the street. Could one of them be trying to get her?

And what about those two people in the ladies' room? Who were they? She was almost sure they were the same ones who'd helped her onto the raft. The incidents seemed unreal, part of an imaginative process that had occurred because she'd been stressed. The only other possibility was ghosts, and she didn't believe in them.

What had the man said? Persons closest to her heart. No one she'd ever worked with, at the Bureau or with Smith-O'Malley, was exactly that. The people closest to her heart were her family. Could one of them . . . ? No. No way. She was getting paranoid. Leaning her elbows on the desk, she put her head in her hands.

"What is it, dear?"

Destiny's head snapped up. "Aunt Cordelia! I didn't hear you come in. Is Tyrrell with you?"

"No, he had some business calls to make." Cordelia sat down opposite Destiny and rubbed her hand over the surface of the desk. "This is a lovely desk. Chestnut, isn't it?"

"Ah, I don't know. It was in the attic. Mrs. Duggan decided all it needed was a good polish." Destiny had the distinct impression her aunt had come on a mission. She'd have to wait her out, though. Cordelia was rarely direct.

"Something's bothering you, Destiny. Would you like to talk about it?"

"Well, I do miss the children."

Cordelia frowned. "They went with Laura. That means we'll never see them. I don't like that."

"Of course you'll see them. Any time you wish. You'll always be welcome here. And we'll come out to California whenever we can—"

"What? Does that mean you're not returning to the business? Tyrrell will be so chagrined. Not that he minds running things, dear. He's never complained."

Destiny's smile twisted. "He's getting a seven-figure salary, Aunt. Why would he complain?"

Her aunt didn't quite frown, but her brows drew together. "I hope you know he earns every penny."

Destiny took a deep breath. "As long as we're on the subject, I should tell you that I've already set everything up so that I can run the business from here. As you know, most of our operation is in out-of-state holdings, both in the Midwest and East—"

"I didn't know," Cordelia said. "Tyrrell doesn't care to speak of business once he's at home."

"But . . . Aunt Cordelia, you have a large block of stock in your name, as does Donald."

"Tyrrell says it's better if he handles both Donald's and my shares. It's more efficient."

Destiny exhaled. She didn't feel her aunt or cousin should let anyone handle their business even if they did have full confidence in Tyrrell. "Very well. I feel that in running such a widespread operation, there's no need for me to remain in California. I'm downsizing many of the operations out there, and pointing us in another direction. It's part of the ten-year plan my father and your late husband had to phase out the regular construction segment and concentrate on equipment needed for outer space exploration. It looks like it could be a bigger market than even they imagined. I intend to retain the main office building in San Francisco. Jobs won't be lost, since a Chicago firm has already made a bid for the segments we're changing. This should bring us into the next millenium in better financial shape."

"You sound like your father." Cordelia blinked. "Tyrrell never mentioned this."

"He might not know. Ryan Cooper—I'm sure you know him; he's chief financial officer—and I handled most of it. The transition should be smooth and the employees will be taken care of by the new company." Before her aunt could reply, she hurried into more explanation. "I also intend to merge much of my operation with Brace's. We'll exchange some personnel and add new ones."

Cordelia whitened. "What of Tyrrell? He likes California, and he's always run the main office."

Destiny steepled her hands. "Actually, since I came on board five years ago, I've taken over many of the responsibilities myself. And Ryan is my right-hand man. I trust Ryan and have known him all my life . . ." Destiny's voice trailed as she felt a cold dampness shiver over her skin. It felt like a warning.

"Yes? Go on, Destiny."

"Ah, yes . . . umm. Much of the corporation is running the way I want it to, and the way I feel it should be."

Cordelia swallowed. "I see. Well then, you must continue to do what you feel is right. I'm sure Tyrrell supports you on this."

"I'm sure he does. My father trusted me to carry on his corporation. I intend to do that."

"Yes, I know. But surely you know that Tyrrell has always done his best to do the same."

"Yes, he has. I talked to Tyrrell about this before I left California. He seemed to understand."

"He never said a word."

"He might've thought you'd be upset."

"And I am." Aunt Cordelia said through tight lips. "I don't know what your father would say about this."

"He'd tell me to go ahead. He always wanted me to take charge."

Cordelia smiled wanly. "You're just like your mother. Lynn was always full steam ahead."

At the mention of her mother, Destiny thought again of the two strangers in the courthouse ladies' room. Without using much effort, she could imagine that the dark-haired woman resembled—in a fuzzy sort of way—her mother. But that was impossible. She didn't believe in ghosts.

Cordelia went on. "Lynn had more energy and enthusiasm than three people put together." Her smile faded. "I remember how much Mason admired that in her."

Destiny frowned. Mason? Her aunt's first husband? Was Cordelia suggesting that Destiny's mother and Cordelia's husband . . . ?

Her shock and confusion must have shown on her face, for Cordelia quickly reassured her.

"No, no," she said. "Nothing happened between Lynn and Mason. Lynn adored your father too much to ever notice another man."

"But Uncle Mason," Destiny said. "He married you, Aunt. He wouldn't have if he hadn't loved you."

Cordelia nodded. "Mason did love me and showed me that love every day. Even knowing that, I couldn't get over my insecurities. I carried a grudge against your mother." Tears welled in her eyes. "I'm so sorry for that. My remorse is like a monkey on my back." Her gaze slid to Destiny. "I never had a girl. I wanted one, another child after Donald. It didn't happen. So you were my girl. You're so like her, so open, so loving. You never see the hatred around you."

The remark bothered Destiny. "Do you?"

Cordelia didn't answer. "It hurt so much when Lynn died. I couldn't tell anyone how I felt, how I'd held in my heart bad thoughts about her, how I felt guilty when she died, as though I'd brought it about."

"Aunt! How could you think such things? My mother was shot in a drive-by shooting. Random violence. Who could know that would happen? Isn't that right?"

Again Cordelia didn't answer. "Then, less than a year later, your father was killed in that elevator accident with Mason. I began to think I was jinxed."

"How could you be responsible for any of it?"

"Then why was I left behind? Alone!" Tears streamed from her eyes, and a muffled sob escaped her. "Sorry." She pulled a lace-edged hanky from her purse and pressed it to her face.

"You have Donald."

Cordelia half laughed, half cried. "Do I? Now he's run off with—with—"

"The woman of his dreams," Destiny said.

Cordelia bit her lip. "You don't think it's a mistake?"

"I think it's wonderful."

Cordelia looked relieved. "I want him to be happy."

"I know that." Destiny felt she and her aunt had crossed a bridge that would have, at one time, seemed uncrossable.

ELEVEN

Brace's parents had invited them for dinner—it was their last night in New York before returning to San Francisco—and Destiny was ambivalent about going. She may have mended fences with her aunt, but she still felt uncomfortable with Susan and John. It didn't help that, as she was dressing, Brace made it clear he'd just as soon spend the evening at home himself—preferably in bed. With some effort, she got both of them out of the house and into his car.

"Once we get our lives in order," he said as he started the engine, we're taking a trip. We're going to Hawaii."

"Are we taking the kids?"

"Yes. We'll tire them out in the water during the day, then I'll tire you out in bed at night."

"Sounds like a plan."

"It is." He steered out of the driveway, glancing

left and right as they passed through the wooded area.

She hadn't been going to say anything. It was foolish, precipitate, and she might be wrong. "I think I might have some good news for you."

"Tell me. I could use some."

"Speaking of the children . . . well, really, speaking of parenthood—"

"Don't tell me you think I wouldn't be a good father," Brace interrupted. "I think I would be."

"I wouldn't argue with that."

"What? You think I'd be a terrific parent?"

"You're jumping the gun."

"Sorry."

"Actually, yes, I think you'd be a great father. You've done well with Jeremy and Ella, and they love being with you. Of course, you've never handled a newborn."

"Neither have you. If we adopt an infant, we can learn together. I'll bet you one great dinner at the new Bird of Paradise restaurant on Kauai I'll be as good as you."

"You're on, mister." She turned in her seat, facing him. "You might get the chance to show your stuff quicker than you think."

"What's that mean?" He pulled onto the highway, the smooth acceleration of the powerful car sounding more like a purring.

"It means I think I've missed my period, or my calendar is wrong."

His hands dropped off the wheel, then snapped

back on again. He steered the car to the side of the highway and stopped. He took a deep breath. "What?"

"I said I missed—"

"I heard it the first time. But it's only been a few weeks." He swallowed, his hands revealing a slight tremor. He turned his head in slow motion. "You're pregnant?"

"I'm not sure."

He leaned toward her, kissing her cheek. "Wow."

"I know. You must be taking the right vitamins."

"Yeah. Or you."

"You're white."

"I'm shocked, happy, stupefied."

"Maybe I should drive."

"All right." He put the car in neutral and got out. Coming around to the passenger side, he opened her door, all but lifting her out. He kissed her, his mouth slanting over hers.

A passing vehicle honked.

"You're wonderful." He led her around to the driver's side, helped her into the seat, fastened her belt. Then, grinning like a Cheshire cat, he went back to the passenger's side and slipped into the seat, fastening his belt. He took her hand and kissed it. "I feel dizzy."

Laughing, Destiny put the car in gear. She looked over at Brace. "All right?"

"Don't think I'll let you get away, Des. I won't."

"You've already told me that."

"Believe it." His smile was slow and steady. "I'm so damned happy."

"So am I. But . . . I'm still not sure."

"I am."

Chuckling, she steered off the shoulder and back onto the curving, hilly highway.

Brace's parents were staying in the same condo Brace had occupied.

Brace had his arm around her as they approached the door.

It was opened by Susan. "There you are. I was watching for you. We were beginning to worry." She studied her son. "Are you ill?"

"No," he said, frowning at her. "I'm pregnant."

Gasping a laugh, his mother shook her head. "You've been drinking. You could've waited—"

"I have not. People don't drink when they're pregnant. It isn't healthy."

Susan glanced at Destiny. "He's on something."

Destiny sighed. "Well, I would've preferred that we didn't do a big announcement before I saw a doctor, but I guess we're past that." Her smile was shy as she faced her mother-in-law. "I think I'm expecting."

Susan's mouth dropped, her eyes lighting up. She grasped Destiny, hugging her. "Oh, I hope I can keep this quiet, but it's so exciting. Three grandchildren in the blink of an eye, so to speak."

Destiny put her arms around Susan, feeling strange. They'd never embraced. Had it been her own uncertainties that had caused the rift that had grown wider through the years? "Maybe not the blink of an eye, but I must say I'm nonplussed at the speed our family is growing."

"Not me," Brace said. "I've been ready for this right along. I could handle six children."

Both Susan and Destiny stared at him.

As though he didn't notice, he preceded them down the short hall to the great room overlooking the lake.

Susan turned to Destiny. "I've something to say."

Feeling her chin rise, Destiny braced herself.

"I've been proud of Brace since he was born. Even before he could walk, he was self-sufficient, into trying anything, taking any dare, climbing the most insurmountable mountain. Nothing ever fazed him for long. He rolled through situations that would've stymied most." She paused, trying to smile and failing. "Then you came along and I knew all of that would change."

"No!" Stunned, Destiny could only stare at Susan. "He's confident, sure of himself. He's smart, good with people, and able to handle any problem in the corporation—"

"He could handle nothing after you left him. He was lifeless, Destiny."

She shook her head. "That's not Brace at all."

Susan nodded. "It is. It was. He needs you like he needs to breathe. Maybe that's why we all took umbrage at your appearance in his life. I wanted to like you, to love you, but I thought I'd lost my son. Both John and I thought that. Only Bel knew your worth."

Her smile appeared, then melted away. "She harangued John and me, excoriating us for not taking you into the family."

"No, no, I never felt left out of the family." Just out of the loop of camaraderie that seemed to vibrate one to the other.

Susan nodded. "Kind of you, but I know you did . . . and we contributed to it." She paused. "Maybe we were jealous because you exuded such power over him." She held up her hand when Destiny opened her mouth. "I mean that in the best way, dear. He loved you . . . loves you to distraction. You took his heart and he doesn't want it back. He only wants you." Susan reached out and hooked the tear that ran down Destiny's cheek. "Oh, don't cry. Please, I don't want you to be unhappy."

"I'm not. I'm—I'm pleased." She put her arms around Susan. "I've wanted to be your friend. I didn't know how."

"Oh, Destiny."

The two women were still embracing when the door behind them opened.

"Hey! What's going on? Mother, you're not picking on Destiny, are you?"

"Bel!"

Destiny and Susan spoke at the same time, whirling toward the speaker.

The three embraced.

Coming up behind them, Donald looked slightly panicked as he realized all three women were crying. "It can't be that bad," he whispered.

"It isn't," his wife informed him. "We're happy."

"Oh."

Destiny grasped his hand and yanked him close to her. "I'm so happy for you guys." She kissed her cousin.

"I'm relieved," Donald said on a sigh, earning a laugh from his new mother-in-law.

"Come over here, Donald. I deserve a kiss."

"You do, indeed." Gracefully he managed to encompass the three women, kissing each one in turn.

"Isn't he wonderful, Mother?" Bel sighed.

Donald blushed.

Destiny laughed.

Susan nodded. "You've done well for yourself, daughter."

TWELVE

"I can't believe you told the whole world about this," Destiny told Brace on the cellular phone in her car.

"I couldn't help it."

"What if the doctor tells me I'm not pregnant?"

"I should be there with you."

"You had to go to that meeting in San Francisco. And you didn't answer my question."

"That's because I'm sure we're pregnant."

Destiny chuckled.

"Call me when you get back to the house."

"I will."

She broke the connection, omitting the information that she was nervous, filled with a worry that she wasn't expecting, while also shaken by the idea that she might, in not so many months, give birth. "What do I know about being a mother?"

Don't be stupid, an inner voice argued. *You've been a mother to Jeremy and Ella.*

Somewhat cheered, she pulled into the parking lot at the hospital. Eying the building where the men had been when she'd visited Divinity, she stemmed a shudder. She hadn't told Brace the doctor's office was in the same building.

The examination and tests seemed to take forever. Back in the doctor's office, Destiny took deep breaths.

Amy Dawson sat behind her desk, grinning. "About seven months from now you should have a baby."

Destiny heard nothing else for at least two minutes.

". . . and just keep to your normal routine. You're in good health."

Blinking, Destiny stammered her thanks and left.

On impulse she decided she would tell Cordelia. If Brace's parents had been there, she would've confirmed it with them too. She stopped at the farmer's market to purchase some fresh fruit for her aunt. Tyrrell had returned to California that morning. Maybe she would invite her aunt to dinner.

Pulling into the parking lot of the huge condominium complex at Blessing Hill, she parked and got out of her car, taking the bag of fruit with her.

Walking over to the door of her aunt's apartment, she pressed the bell, listening as it chimed through the place. When there was no answer, she rang again. Still nothing. Without thinking, she put her hand on the door handle. When it turned and the door swung back, she was surprised. "Aunt Cordelia?" she called.

It wasn't until she was in the narrow foyer that she saw the message on the door. *Gone shopping*, the note said in her aunt's precise handwriting. *Will return in two hours*. Her time of departure and return were on the note. She wouldn't be back for a while.

Thinking to leave a note, Destiny walked through to the kitchen and placed the grapes and cantaloupe in a wooden fruit dish.

"Pencil," she muttered. "Where is the—"

The phone rang, interrupting the conversation with herself. Deciding to let the answering machine handle it, she retraced her steps, still looking for a paper and pencil so she could write a note. As she stepped into the small office, the answering machine came on, catching her attention. "It's Kimberley. I'm in my new office. Tyrrell, I hope you're still there. I need to speak to you. We have a glitch here and we should discuss it. Cordelia, in case Tyrrell has already left for California, please tell him it's important that we touch base as soon as possible. Beaucoup important." She gave an extension, then said thanks and hung up.

Destiny stared at the machine. Kimberley. Would that be Donald's friend? If she was so desperate to talk to someone, why hadn't she contacted Ryan? And why had she left that number? That extension belonged to her office, and was used by her and her personal staff only.

Frowning, she left the condo, forgetting the note, mulling over the news that Kimberley—what was her last name?—not only worked for the corporation, but used her office. She drove home, her focus on the California office.

As soon as she entered the house, she was confronted by Mrs. Duggan.

"Sit down and have some tea," the housekeeper ordered. "I made some biscuits. None of that junk in 'em either. Now that you're eating for two, you need to keep your strength up."

Agape, Destiny stared at her. "How did you know?"

"Easy. Had a few myself. All grown up. They have their families now, and I don't want to leave Yokapa County and live anywhere else."

"Oh."

"Sit."

"All right." Destiny took a cup of tea and a biscuit. "That would make me feel better."

"Course it would. Made right. Not store boughten."

Destiny nodded.

"The mister called. Said you was to call him."

Destiny dabbed at her mouth. "I'll do it now. Then I'll want to speak to the children, so I'll probably be in the library for some time."

"Don't worry, I'll call you for dinner."

"Thank you."

"Don't mention it."

Destiny scampered out of the kitchen and down the hall.

"And stop that foolish running. You're a woman grown and a mother-to-be. Behave," Mrs. Duggan called after her.

"Sorry," Destiny muttered, slowing her pace.

Closing the library door behind her, she dialed Brace's private number at his office. It was picked up on the first ring.

"Des?"

"Yes."

"Well?"

"You're going to be a papa," she said.

"Damn! I love it. What does the doctor say about you?"

"Healthy as a horse. I'm on a vitamin regimen, the whole bit."

"I'll be home later this evening. I already have a plane reservation."

"Brace, that wasn't necessary. Are you sure you should?"

"Yes. I want to get back to you as soon as I can. Twenty-four hours away from you is more than I can stand."

"Good. I want you here." Thinking of the baby made her recall her visit to her aunt's condominium. "Oh, by the way, you're good with names."

"Sometimes. Why?"

"Do you recall that friend of Donald's?"

"Kimberley Marchese?"

"That's it. Marchese. I know this sounds weird, but she's using my office at Smith-O'Malley."

He paused. "Why she'd need to use your office, I can't figure."

"Neither could I. I don't even know her, and I find out she's inhabiting my office."

"This is bothering you."

"Yes. We can talk about it when you get home."

"Okay, love, I'll be leaving soon. I miss you."

"I miss you too."

"Hold that thought."

"I will."

"By the way, it's in the works to move the Mendez-Coolidge headquarters east. I thought you might like to hear that."

"I do, I do. I can't believe you could move so fast."

"I'm anxious to be with my wife. Desperate men can move mountains."

Destiny was still smiling when she hung up the phone. She sat there for a moment, then picked up the phone again and dialed Ryan Cooper's direct line at the office in San Francisco. The phone rang several times before he answered. "Ryan? It's Des." She paused, frowning. "You sound funny."

"I've been fired."

Destiny straightened in her chair. "Don't be ridiculous."

"I'm not. Your uncle sent me a memo, accusing me of skimming company funds. I was shown copies of data that seem to back it up."

"Listen to me. Are you paying attention?"

"Yes."

Destiny didn't like the dull sound of his voice. "I'll be out there as soon as I can catch a flight. I'll book it right away. I'll stay with you and Damian, if that's all right. It's still morning there. With luck I should be there by dinnertime."

"Des, don't. I'll go quietly."

"No. You won't. I'm relying on you to handle the office out there. You and I know that. Contact the board for me. I'm calling an emergency meeting for tomorrow morning. Do it, Ryan."

"You mean it? You're not going to investigate—"

"There's nothing to investigate. I know you. My uncle doesn't. I'll take care of Uncle Tyrrell. Just make sure you gather the board."

"I'll do it."

"Good. I'll see you soon. I'll call from the plane with my arrival time. Can you meet me?"

"Of course."

Destiny broke the connection, then redialed. There was no answer on Brace's private line. She left a message, then another one on her machine. She called for reservations, then called Divinity.

"You mean you're flying out now?"

"Right." Destiny gave her the itinerary. "If you or Jake can intercept Brace, I'd appreciate it. I'm grabbing a shuttle to Syracuse, then a jet from there to California. With luck and a tail wind I'll be in San Francisco this evening and in the office tomorrow morning."

"Your hubby might not like it."

"I'm sure he won't. It can't be helped."

"Good luck. I'll tell Dynasty. Between the four of us we'll handle this end."

"Thanks."

Less than an hour later she was on the shuttle to Syracuse, and after that on the private jet that would take her cross-country.

On the flight, she managed to get more information faxed to her from Ryan. She couldn't believe the mountain of evidence against her friend. It hardened her resolve to get to the bottom of it and clear his name. Ryan had been hired by her father, and Porter had been grooming the younger man for a high-powered job when he died. Ten years her senior and extraordinarily savvy about business, Ryan had been invaluable to her when she'd taken over. More than that, he and his partner Damian had become her close friends.

She managed to nap part of the way, but she was still a little tired when they landed in San Francisco.

She was almost through the barriers when she saw Damian Scinter. "What's wrong?" she asked as soon as she reached him.

He took her flight bag. "Nothing sinister. Ryan thought he should stay on the job."

She glanced up at her artistic looking friend. "They've been putting him through the mill the past couple of months, haven't they?"

Damian nodded. "They have. Front, back, and sideways. He didn't want to involve you because he knew about the fragile deal going on between you and Brace."

Destiny took his arm and squeezed. "How'd you like to be a godfather?"

Damian nearly dropped her bag. "Are you enceinte, love?"

"I am."

"Then Ryan and I will insist on being the godparents."

"Good. I don't want anyone else." Her smile stiffened to a frown. "And Ryan is staying on the job. We've got a board meeting in the morning."

"Pulling out the stops, are we?"

"Damn straight. This company was put in my care, and I picked the best man to help me run it. I'm fond of my uncle, but he can't do this. Once I set him straight, it won't happen again." She caught Damian's scowl. "What? You don't think I can do it?"

"I think you'll try, but there seems to be a great deal of undercutting going on—"

"I intend to stop all the crap going on, overt or covert, and let the board and everyone else know how the company will be run. This corporation will operate to the specifications set down by my father and reinforced by his friends on the board."

Damian hesitated. "They're getting older, Des. Sometimes it's easier to give way."

"Not for this gal, and they'd better know it."

His grin was slow in coming. "How did I forget how tough you can be? If you're cornered, you come out with guns blazing. If anyone can set this straight, you can. I'll help, even though I don't know what I can do."

"You're not just a wonderful artist, Damian, love. You're also a bit of a hacker. I remember that tidbit of information you once let drop."

"Hey, don't start something that'll land us in jail."

"I don't think it'll go that far. I just need some information."

"You don't *think* it'll go that far? I'm not reassured." He led her to the parking garage. "But I'm with you, as Ryan and I have always been."

"No one knows I'm here except you and Ryan, right?"

He opened the door of a new Mercedes, nodding. "Just as you requested, *Oberleutnant*."

"Very funny." When Damian started the engine, she leaned over and patted his arm. "I feel good about this. I'm going to win."

"I, for one, have never doubted you, not since you tackled that football player when we foolishly got ourselves in the middle of a bar brawl."

"He was a sucker for a right."

"Plus you happen to be a master of judo, not to mention all that spectacular FBI training."

"Hey, he didn't know that."

"You were always too intrepid."

"Not really. You would've handled it if there hadn't been two of them. I evened the odds, that's all."

Damian laughed. "I love you, lady."

"I know. That's why you're going to be a godfather, you and Ryan."

Brace looked out the window of the plane, glaring at the fluffy clouds. The rising sun behind them cast beautiful shadows, a rainbow spectrum.

"Sir? Could I get you something to drink?"

"Hemlock, straight up."

"I beg your pardon?"

"Just coffee, please." He couldn't believe he was on a plane again, flying *back* to San Francisco. He'd called Destiny from the air the previous evening, only to get the answering machine and her message informing him she'd left for California herself to take care of a business crisis. Then he'd talked to the Blessings and found out she'd called a board meeting! Dammit, she was expecting. "Fat chance she'd back down."

"I beg your pardon, sir?"

"It's nothing. I'm on my way to a fight."

The flight attendant, blinked, gave him a nervous smile and the coffee.

Fuming, he took the coffee and gulped it, nearly searing his tongue. His wife was driving him nuts. What made her think he'd let her handle whatever it was she was trying to handle on her own? They were going to have a talk!

❖————————————❖

She'd stayed with Ryan and Damian and had a good night's sleep. When she entered their kitchen the next morning, she smiled at Ryan. "You look awful."

Damian grinned. Ryan scowled, his freckled, cherubic features twisted. He was as tall as Damian, but more muscular. He had a serene mien that hid a sharp, incisive mind.

"What did you expect? What the hell do you think you're going to accomplish with this board meeting?"

"Did you call Farrars?"

"I did. The entire battery of lawyers, plus their account investigators, will be on campus today."

"Campus? Is that what we're calling the corporation now?" Damian asked, handing Destiny a large orange juice. "I took the vitamins from your bag."

She smiled her thanks.

"It feels like Kent State at the moment," Ryan said, gloom and doom in his tone. He stared at his orange juice as though it had been drained from his carburetor. "You could ruin the corporation, Des."

"Uh-uh. Pass the toast, please, and I'd like more jam."

"You're not eating for quintuplets, Des, just one," Ryan said. "You should never have come out here when you're pregnant."

"I'm fine. The doctor said so. This child is cemented within for the duration."

"Don't sound so cocky."

"Then don't sound so gloomy."

Damian laughed, earning a glare from his room-mate.

"I'm handling everything," Destiny said. "I'm my father's daughter. I know what I'm doing."

Ryan rounded on her. "What if there is someone undercutting the place? It damn well looks that way. If so, there could be nasty repercussions. You'd be the logical target, Des." He banged the counter with the flat of his hand. "So help me Hannah, if you've put yourself in any type of danger—"

"That's why I have you and Damian."

Ryan growled. Damian winced.

"Drink your orange juice. I want to get moving," Des instructed.

Damian grimaced. "I didn't think about the danger. You shouldn't be here, Des. Let us handle it."

"Handle what?" She took a bite of jam and toast and closed her eyes. "Good."

"Anything that could hurt you. It never occurred to me."

"Well, it should have," Ryan shouted.

"Stop it," Destiny ordered. "There's no big conspiracy. There's been fudging at best, maybe even just a computer error. We'll settle it, you'll be back on the job, and I'll be on my way back to Yokapa County."

Ryan slumped against the counter, setting down his glass and sighing. "I hope you're right."

"I am. Pass the jam, please, and hurry. I want to

be down there before anyone else. Everyone's coming?"

Ryan nodded, nudging the jar toward her.

Brace stared up at the building that housed Des's company. "She's too damned intrepid for her own good."

His father, who'd picked Brace up at the airport, chuckled. "That's why you love her."

Brace grimaced. "Let's get in there. If I know Des, she'll be in place already."

They entered the lobby and were at once spotted by a guard, who approached, scowling.

"What's going on?" John whispered. "An inordinate amount of caution, wouldn't you say? Do you know this guard?"

"No, but I'm not going to argue with him." Brace smiled when the guard asked if he was a board member. Since he and his father were, and they produced identification, they were let through the barrier.

Brace ignored the bank of elevators and went right to the one used by Des or her chief financial officer, Ryan. No one else had a key. He used the one she'd given him shortly after their marriage. It worked.

Neither man spoke as they ascended to the executive floor and the main suite of offices.

When the doors opened, Brace took a breath and exited in front of his father. He didn't know what he expected to find, certainly not an attractive blond woman in her late thirties seated at Destiny's desk. "Good morning," he said smoothly.

"I . . . ah . . . yes . . . Good morning. I assume you're here for the board meeting." She rose, smoothing her hands down the front of her suit. "I'm afraid I don't know all the board members yet." She approached them, holding out her right hand. "I'm Kimberley Marchese."

Well, well, Brace thought. "Brace Coolidge," he said, taking her hand.

Blood rushed to her face, and she barely restrained herself from snatching her hand back. After a moment he released her.

"And my father, John."

"I—I don't think either of you were expected," she said.

"Obviously." He jingled his set of keys in his hand. "I'll lock up behind you," he said, brandishing the keys.

She stiffened. "This office is generally left open."

"Not when Destiny's not here." He saw the argument gathering in her eyes, the struggle to tamp it down, the swallowing of bile.

A smile touched her lips and fell off as she inclined her head. "Then I shall see you at the board meeting."

Hiding his surprise, he cocked an eyebrow. "My father and I will be there, since we are members. Will you be taking notes?"

"My presence has been requested."

Brace wondered about that. He took a risk and said, "I'm sure this meeting will be closed to non-members." As she flushed again, he knew he'd hit a nerve. He caught his father's low cough. "I'm sure you'll excuse us." He waited until she exited, then looked at his father.

"You don't like her, I presume," John said.

"I don't know her. That's the first time I've seen her. But I've heard some things about her, and I sure don't like her in Destiny's chair."

John nodded. "And you're concerned about Destiny. Just don't let that spark your temper."

"You're right," Brace said between his teeth. "Thank God I finally got in touch with one of Destiny's VP's and found out what happened. I can't believe Ryan was fired; she'll want to know all the details concerning that. Ryan is one of her closest friends. She trusts him."

"So who do we kill? Or is that whom?"

Brace unbent, giving his father a sour smile. "Okay, I'm burned. And I could beat the tar out of the person who started the brouhaha with Ryan. That was bound to get Destiny fired up, and yes, I'm angry with my wife. I'm also worried about her."

"That's not news."

Brace stared at his father. "She's taken me into her life again, Dad, but I can't prove I wasn't unfaithful."

John grasped his arm. "Listen to me, son. I'm

sure in her heart she believes you." He paused. "I also know when you love someone very much, you're vulnerable. She is, so are you. You can't fight that. Just realize that some things you have to take on faith. Dutch comfort, maybe, but the truth."

Brace nodded. "I'm still going to ferret out who tried to come between us." He glanced at his watch. "We'd better get to the boardroom." His gaze slid to the desk. "Wait. I want to see if I can find out why Kimberley Marchese was in here." He walked around the desk and sat down, studying its surface. Seeing a letter opener lying in front of him, he leaned back and stared at the middle drawer. Destiny always kept it locked. There were marks on it that looked as though they'd been made by someone trying to force it open. He jerked it. Still locked.

"Interrupt a break-in?" his father asked.

"Maybe. I think I'll run a check on that lady." He picked up the phone and dialed. "This is Brace Coolidge. Tell Webb I want some background run on Kimberley Marchese." He relayed all the information he had, then broke the connection. "Now we'll face the meeting."

"Why do I have the feeling I've been invited to brawl?"

Brace's laugh was harsh. "Fasten your seat belt."

"Wish I'd brought my brass knuckles."

Brace put his hand on his father's shoulder. "Did I mention that I prefer having you at my back?"

"Thanks. I feel the same."

They strode down the hall, not breaking stride to speak to anyone. More than one curious glance skated off them.

"I think my daughter-in-law is planning a siege."

"She's not afraid of a fight, damn her hide."

THIRTEEN

Destiny tapped the gavel once used by her father. Looking down the long table from one side to the other, she noted two seats were empty. She'd expected that. She was about to speak when the door opened.

"Sorry we're late," Brace said.

"Hello, everyone," John said. "How are you, Des?"

"Fine, sir," she responded, her voice faint.

John moved to one of the vacant chairs.

Brace lifted the other one and carried it across the room, placing it next to Destiny's. "Hi."

"Hi."

"You were about to begin, I think."

"Ah, yes . . . begin. Good idea." She looked at the papers on the table, her mind a blank. Then she glanced up at the expectant faces, wondering why she was there.

Damian, sitting behind her, coughed. Destiny had explained to the board that he was assisting her with the current business crisis. Ryan Cooper sat next to him. He grimaced at Damian, shaking his head.

Damian shrugged. The board had been told he was there to take notes. He was doing that by using a tape recorder. He coughed again.

"Ah, yes," Destiny said. "I want to thank everyone for coming on such short notice. As was mentioned, this is a very important meeting. We need to straighten out a glitch or two that could cause us problems in the future." She cleared her throat and shuffled the papers in front of her, not looking at Brace but quite sure he was studying her. "Much to my surprise, I was informed yesterday that my trusted associate Ryan Cooper, chief financial officer for Smith-O'Malley, was being separated from the corporation—"

"Not without good cause, my dear," Tyrrell interrupted, his tone soothing. "We wanted to spare you the embarrassment and hurt of discovering how betrayed you'd been by a trusted friend—"

Destiny held up her hand, silencing her uncle. "Please. I don't need any corroboration of the tale. I looked up everything to do with this fiasco." She stared at her uncle, then, one by one, each member of the board. "The findings are bogus and untruthful—"

"Destiny! My dear—"

"I'm sorry, Uncle. I know you were convinced by

this flimsy evidence, but I can tell you it's all counterfeit and I can prove it."

She gestured to Damian to pass around the sheets they'd compiled. "As you can see by the stats in front of you, it would've been impossible for Ryan to have accomplished the stated larcenies. In almost every case, he was either out of the city or out of the country. In the other situations, he'd already written memos closing down the operations from which the money was siphoned. We're still not sure why they went forward, but we'll discover that too. Other simpler projects that were fouled or went belly up were not given to the right individuals. It looks like a snafu in communications. Lack of experience was a factor in some of this." She looked up. "Those thought to be innocent because the scope was too large for their expertise will be retrained, not fired." She coughed to clear her throat. "If there was deliberate sabotage—"

Gasps and protests interrupted her.

"—that will be dealt with also. We're not sure who engineered this. We're working on it. As for Ryan, he will continue running the West Coast office, as I will oversee the entire operation from New York." She leaned forward, placing her forearms on the conference table. "There will be an auditing—" Choked protests broke her speech. She continued. "—not just because it is the wisest way for us to proceed with a financial investigation, but because it's the logical way for an outfit of our size and scope to begin—"

"What of contracts already in operation?" interrupted Mr. Willard Wilkins, one of her father's oldest friends. "Won't that give the company a bad name? Won't some want to pull in their invoices, or even cancel?"

"Not necessarily. I don't intend to put this in *Forbes* magazine. This will be a thorough but private cleansing and examination of the business. This will not only clear Ryan's good name but will also solidify my position as head of this corporation."

Mr. Wilkins sat back in his chair, smiling. "You're Smitty's daughter, all right. For some time I've worried about that."

Destiny smiled at him. "I'm tough enough, sir."

She took a deep breath, slanting a glance at Brace, who was slouched back in his chair, watching her. He was smiling!

Buoyed and energized, she lifted her chin. "Since I am the majority stockholder in this corporation, I move we reinstate Ryan Cooper." She smiled when it was done by unanimous voice vote. "Thank you. It's in the minutes and so on record.

"As chief executive officer of this corporation," she went on, "I will continue to oversee the operations that meant so much to my family. The day-to-day running of the business will be handled by Ryan Cooper. I don't have to list his qualifications, or how much faith my family has in him. I will say this about my friend. He's the most qualified person to head up this corporation and I trust him."

Brace saw Ryan's bug-eyed stare as he watched

Destiny, and grinned. She'd surprised him. She'd delighted her husband. She'd be with him more. She'd all but said she wouldn't have to be jaunting back and forth to California. He fully intended to leave a good share of his operations to his executives and officers. He'd oversee it all from Yokapa County, New York.

Pulling himself back from his musings, he focused on Destiny.

". . . which will fully incorporate all the present needs of the corporation and address what will be called for in the near future."

When she finished speaking, there was a silence, then one by one the board members commented, almost all solidly with her.

Tyrrell was the last to speak. "You know I will always be in your corner, my dear, though I am of a more conservative bent than you."

Destiny smiled and nodded. "I think we can adjourn this meeting except to congratulate the new CFO, and ourselves, because he'll be back on the job." She turned to a red-faced Ryan and shook his hand.

"Des," he managed to say.

"Don't thank me. Not necessary. I picked the best man, twice." She kissed his cheek and turned to Brace.

"Well done." He took her in his arms and kissed her.

"Are you miffed?" she asked, leaning back to look at him.

"I was. Not now. You'll be home with me in

Yokapa County where you belong. Ryan will be happy running this place—"

"And boring me," Damian interjected, "with all the details of his long- and short-range plans, ad infinitum, ad nauseam." He rolled his eyes.

Ryan laughed, rubbing his hands in exuberance. The smile left his face when Tyrrell appeared in front of him. "Ah, sir, I—"

"My boy, I'm happy for you. My staff will be at your disposal."

Destiny frowned, edging out of Brace's hold. "That reminds me, Uncle. Kimberley Marchese was using the phone in my office the other day. She's not on my staff, and I want only them in my office."

Tyrrell stiffened. "I have no idea why she was there. I will certainly speak to her about it. If you insist, I can let Kimberley go."

"No, no. Don't fire her. It's not a problem. I'd just rather be dealing with my own staff."

Tyrrell exhaled. "I'll see to it."

Destiny patted his arm. "I know everything has been very chaotic recently. Just be glad that Donald is so happy."

"There is that." He sighed. "Though I was taken aback when Donald and Bel eloped."

"So was I," John Coolidge said, clapping Tyrrell on the back. "I will say this, Tyrrell. My daughter has never looked happier in her life. I can't begrudge her such joy. Why don't we all go out to dinner and discuss this expanding family of ours?"

"That's a great idea," Destiny said, as Brace was shaking his head in a firm negative.

"When am I going to be alone with you?" he whispered in her ear.

"Tonight when we get home from dinner. I want to get back to Yokapa County as soon as possible, but I think I'll wait a couple of days and help Ryan where I can."

Brace shrugged. "Suits me. I've got a few knots to tie at my place. It'll work." When she smiled at him, he groaned and kissed her again. "I need you," he whispered.

"Ditto." She reached up and kissed his cheek.

"Are we in the way?" Ryan inquired.

"Yes," Brace snapped, making Destiny and Ryan laugh.

"You'll feel better with a good dinner in you," John said.

"That's not where my hunger lies," Brace muttered, earning himself a look from Destiny.

She hooked her hand in Brace's arm. "I've asked Ryan and Damian to be godparents to our children."

"All three?"

"Three?" Damian gulped.

Destiny patted his hand as they left the boardroom. "Don't worry. I've explained everything to Ryan."

"Comforting." Damian rolled his eyes. "Three," he muttered. "Why can't she do anything in a simple way?"

Dinner was relaxing and enjoyable, with everyone

tacitly agreeing to steer the conversation away from business. It was late by the time Destiny and Brace were in his car, heading toward the home they had shared.

"You'll get arrested driving at this speed," she said mildly. He didn't answer, merely gave her a look that could have melted metal. He didn't slow down until they reached the house.

"Finally," he said as he helped her out of the car. "I thought we'd never get here."

They walked up the path to the narrow, high house on Lombard Street.

As Brace opened the door, she hesitated, her gaze shifting from the entry hall to him. When he started to ask if something was wrong, she at last stepped past him into the house.

"It's not you, Brace. It's me," she said by way of explanation. "Something was broken between us when I left this house." Her smile twisted. "It's silly to be . . . superstitious."

He shut the door, then put his arm around her, holding her close. "No, you're being wary. I'm the same. We've come a long way this summer, Des. We're hitting the autumn full speed with a family. We want to safeguard it, not let anything harm it."

She nodded, her face pressed to his chest.

"Welcome home, Mrs. Coolidge."

Brace groaned. "Dammit."

Destiny lifted her head. "Hedges, how are you?"

"Fine, ma'am. You were missed."

Brace grimaced at the older man, who had been

working for the Coolidge family since Brace was a preschooler. "Go to bed."

"No," Hedges answered.

Destiny laughed. "How are the short stories coming?"

"Great. Sold one to a mystery magazine."

"Wonderful. Keep it up."

"Yeah," Brace grumbled. "I'm ecstatic."

"Grumpy, isn't he? Bad dinner?"

"Yes," Brace snapped.

"It wasn't. It was delicious. We started with—"

"Forget the menu," Brace interrupted, scooping her into his arms.

"Good night, Hedges," Destiny said over Brace's shoulder.

"Good night, ma'am," Hedges said, laughing.

Brace strode up the stairs to their room, kicking the door shut behind him. "I had a long talk with your doctor. She assured me there's no danger in lovemaking."

"You had a long talk with my doctor?"

"Yes. Very important. I've listed all the foods that are most beneficial, the right drinks at the right time of day, that sort of thing."

"Tell me you didn't keep her on the phone for this."

"Of course I did. Right after you called me and told me she'd confirmed the pregnancy."

"Oh Lord, the doctor is going to hate me."

Brace studied her while he undressed her.

"That's foolish. I impressed on her that we were going to take every care."

"I'm sure she loved that."

"Well, she didn't say." He kissed her toes. "You have the nicest feet."

"Don't tell me. Now that I'm pregnant you've developed a foot fetish."

"No. At least I don't think I have." He threw off his clothes and got into bed beside her, moving close to her. "I admit to having a fetish about you."

"That's fine."

He grinned and kissed her. "I love you so much." In the middle of saying it, he yawned.

Destiny laughed. "That round trip east and west and no rest." She slid her arms around his neck.

"How poetic. I'm still making love to you." When his mouth moved down her body, she shook with want. "I'll always need you and our kids."

"Me too," she whispered.

He blew on her middle, letting his tongue intrude into her navel. When she groaned, Brace smiled. Arousing her was more important than being aroused by her. It had always been that way. Of course, his generosity was always rewarded: The moment he aroused her, he went out of his mind with desire.

"You're everything to me," he muttered against her middle.

"I feel the same. I'm so glad we're together. I wasn't complete without you, Brace."

"Me either."

"We have a family and it's growing bigger. I've never been so happy."

"It's wonderful."

"I've never wanted anyone but you."

He kissed her thighs, letting his mouth run down each leg, tickling her behind the knees. When she trembled, he worked his way up to her breasts, ministering to each one, laving her neck with his tongue, then prodding her ears in the same rhythm as he would her lower body.

When she writhed against him, he fought the surge that coursed his body.

Over and over he made love to her with his mouth and tongue. When he finally used them to bring her to culmination, he came as well.

Moments later, holding her close, he heard her chuckle.

"Don't rub it in, Des. I made an ass of myself."

She turned, kissing his chest. "You didn't. You responded to our shared sexuality."

"Like a hound dog." He should've had more control. He hadn't had an orgasm like that since his teenage years.

His gloomy tone made her laugh. "I love you. Let's take a shower."

"Then we change the bed," he told her, a reluctant laugh pulled from him when she went into gales. "You're making fun of me. Not fair."

"I can do it. I love you."

"I love you, too," he said as he bent down to kiss her.

FOURTEEN

Destiny woke and for a moment was startled to find herself in her old bedroom in San Francisco. The sensation was painful, then she remembered everything and turned, smiling.

Brace was lying close to her, his lips parted, breathing in a slow, regular cadence, locked into deep sleep. She wasn't about to waken him.

Lying there, she thought over the past few days, all that she'd accomplished. Many things still puzzled her. She still didn't know who had instigated the problems at Smith-O'Malley or why Ryan had been the fall guy. She needed some answers. Where to start?

The office, was the sensible answer.

She glanced again at her sleeping husband. He'd been exhausted the night before, even prior to their lovemaking, and she didn't expect him to awaken any time soon. He'd probably still be asleep by the time she got back.

Slipping free of his hold was an aerobic exercise, but she finally managed. She took a quick shower, donned a sweater and jeans that were already a little tight, and headed downstairs. When she reached the foyer, Hedges was there.

"It's tea, juice, wheat cereal, and bananas for you."

Destiny blanched. "I won't eat it all."

"You will and you won't be ill."

She smiled, not believing him, but realizing it did no good to argue. In fact, she ate a good bit, and was pleased that so far she had not suffered from morning sickness. By the time she was through, Hedges had disappeared into the basement. He had an office down there, and she was loath to disturb him. She'd be back in under an hour anyway.

She left the house and walked across the shallow fenced yard that was almost all garden, and into the detached three-car garage.

Driving the streets of San Francisco brought a smile to her face. She'd always loved the city, though she would be leaving it behind with no regrets. Her life was in the East now.

The drive didn't take long. Even though there was traffic, it was nothing like the weekday snarls. She pulled into the underground garage, waved to the attendant, whom she didn't know, and parked in her usual place.

As she crossed the lobby to her private elevator,

she noticed no one. The security guard must be making his rounds, she thought. Ascending, she leaned back against the wall, glad of the privacy. It helped that the lift opened directly into her office. She smiled, thinking of her mother and father, who always worked together in the privacy of the large office. To Destiny it was almost homey, redolent of sweet memories. She could inhale and feel her parents beside her. That thought brought others, like a row of dominoes falling. Were those people who had saved her in the lake, who had warned her at the courthouse, her parents? It seemed less and less bizarre to believe that. The elevator doors opened and she put the ponderings on hold.

Dropping her keys and purse on her desk, she looked around the office, wondering where to begin. Her gaze fell first on her computer, a logical place to start, but then, as if drawn by some unseen power, her gaze lifted to her bookshelves. Specifically to one volume that held the collected works of Shakespeare and another, on the shelf below that, titled *Three Plays*, by Sean O'Casey. Her parents' safe hid behind those books. How many years had it been since she'd opened it? Maybe it had answers.

She pushed at the Shakespeare volume, then the O'Casey. Shakespeare-O'Casey marked Smith-O'Malley. Clever. Grinning, she watched the door camouflaged by books open. She spun the dial—the combination was her birthday—and the door popped open. Inside was a small journal and a loose-leaf notebook. She frowned. She thought there had been more. It seemed unlikely that these books, put there by her parents several years ago, would have any answers.

Taking them to the desk, she opened the notebook. Cold shivered over her, making her look up. Blinking, she stared at the two people standing in the middle of her office, seemingly encased in an aureole.

"Hello," she said hesitantly. "Are . . . are you my mother and father?" Had they nodded? Smiled? "What's wrong?"

"Grave danger, my dear," the woman said. "You must study the world around you. We can't protect you. You must do it yourself."

"Wait! Don't go. Tell me what I need to know."

"Read," they said in chorus.

Destiny looked down at the material in front of her. "All right, but this doesn't look like much." She glanced up and no one was there. Leaning forward, elbows on the desk, she exhaled. "Am I crazy or what? I choose to believe that you are my parents. I don't care how crazy that seems." She looked around the office. "Thanks for being here."

Sighing, she bent over the notebook. She was soon engrossed. It looked to her as though six years earlier, before her mother died, Smith-O'Malley had suffered some of the same sort of financial irregularities she'd discovered that week. Her mother had been investigating them.

Engrossed as she was, she didn't hear the door open. She wasn't sure if it was a sound or a sense that brought her out of her intense concentration. She looked up, startled. Two people stood just inside the door. She recognized the man—Roger Curlew, her uncle's personal assistant—but the woman was a stranger. Instinct told her, though, that she was Kimberley Marchese.

"I'm busy," she said. "Would you please leave?"

The woman shrugged. "Sorry, but no."

Destiny threw down her pen. "Look. Let me make it plainer. Get the hell out of my office."

"No," Roger said softly.

Destiny stared at Kimberley and Roger, a frisson of fear running down her spine. She cleared her throat. "All right. What is it?"

"We have a few questions for you."

"Ask. And by the way, I have a question of my own. How did you know I was here?"

"Tindoni, the guard in the parking garage, is in our pay."

"What are you talking about?" It didn't bode well for her, whatever it was. Roger didn't answer. His gaze skated around the room, landing on the open safe. "My, my, what have we here? I'd better check."

Instinct had Destiny rising, scooping up the notebook and journal, depositing them in the safe, and shutting it in one swift motion, the books concealing the door as though it had never been.

She turned to face Roger. "Back off," she told him. His twisted smile had her skin in goose bumps.

"You heard me." She felt threatened, shaken. "Get out of my way. Better yet, get out of my office."

"Open it," he demanded.

She shook her head. She had to get back to her desk. The silent alarm button Ryan had insisted on having installed was there. It would send signals to the police, to her house, to security, to Ryan. "Out of my way."

"Open it." He lifted his fist.

"Can't until I get to the desk."

Roger moved aside.

From the corner of her eye, Destiny saw her uncle enter the office, open his mouth, lift his hand. She dove for the desk, reaching for the button, pressing it. "Uncle, look out!"

Something hit the back of her head. She fell, thinking of her parents, of Brace, of her unborn child.

Brace rolled over and looked up into Ryan's face. "What the hell . . . ?" Sleep dazed he looked over to where Destiny should have been. "Damn! Where is she? Why are you here?" Yawning, he rubbed his face, then straightened, wide awake. "Is something wrong?"

"I don't know. That's why I'm here. I called to talk to Destiny and Hedges said she'd left. He figured she went to the office. I called there. A security guard answered. He was evasive. I brought his record up on the computer. I didn't hire—"

Just then the red light started blinking on the console next to the bed, accompanied by a whining sound.

Brace cursed. Ryan whitened.

"Dammit! That's her office alarm."

"That means trouble."

Brace almost knocked Ryan over when he leaped out of bed. He threw clothes on. "I have to call Webb. Somebody has to get over there, and fast."

"Damian's already on his way over there."

"Let's go." Brace sprinted out the door and down the stairs, passing Hedges in the foyer. "Call Webb—"

"Did that when Ryan arrived," Hedges said. "I'll go with you."

"No! Stay here. Coordinate things. Call my father—"

"Did that."

Brace nodded, then raced down the hall to the back door.

"The Mercedes is running," Hedges called after him.

"I love that man," Ryan muttered. "My car's on the street. Keys in it—"

"Hedges will handle it. Get in."

The car shot out into the narrow alley, speeding down the wrong way to the entrance. "Quicker this way," Brace said to Ryan.

Ryan held on. "Gotcha."

❖━━━━━━❖

Damian Scinter scowled as he reached the Smith-O'Malley office building. Whatever was Des doing at the office on a Saturday? She was pregnant, for pity's sake. He was about to turn into the parking garage when instinct had him turning down a side street and parking there. He wasn't sure why, but he had a sense something was wrong, and it would be best if he could get to Destiny's office without running into anyone. To that end, rather than walking around to the main entrance, he used a side door that Ryan generally preferred. He had given Damian a key.

Once inside, he felt foolish for not using the front door, yet he couldn't shake the feeling that stealth was called for. Reaching an inner safety door, he tried it. Locked. Again the key worked. He thought he was home free, until a man called out behind him.

"Hey! What're you doing? You're not one of Mr. Curlew's people, are you?"

"Yes, I am." Damian turned and saw that he had entered the building just down the hall from the main entrance, and that the security guard there had spotted him. The hefty guard was striding toward him. "Check it out."

He followed the guard to the security desk. When the man turned, Damian picked up the heavy flashlight that sat there and brought it down on the guard's head.

"Actually," he murmured, "I work for myself." He winced when he looked at the prone figure. He wasn't even sure why he'd thought it necessary to do that. Destiny would probably kill him for roughing up her staff. What if she wasn't even there?

He stared at the bank of elevators, then past that to the small private one. That might be best. The doors that opened onto Destiny's office could be controlled so that they wouldn't open unless he pressed a certain button. There was also a small window he could look through. If she wasn't there, he'd retreat in good order, and pray that the guard wouldn't come to until he'd left the complex.

The elevator came to a silent halt. Taking a deep breath, certain he'd find her office empty, he looked out the small square window. Blinking, not believing his eyes, he saw Destiny on the floor and the back of someone leaving her office. Was that the Mr. Curlew the guard had mentioned? Why had he left Destiny there? She was pregnant, dammit!

When the office door closed, Damian opened the elevator doors. He watched the other door for several seconds, but when it wasn't reopened, he rushed across the office to Destiny. "Des? Des, baby, you're not hurt, are you? Open your eyes," Damian whispered. "Hurry. We have to get out of here."

It seemed to take forever, then her eyelids fluttered.

"Come on, come on. I won't let you be hurt."

She opened her eyes. "Da-Damian? Wha—?"

"No time. Is it all right if I lift you? You're not bleeding or anything, are you?"

"I don't think so. My head hurts." He helped her to her feet, and she leaned on him as they made their way to the elevator. "So the alarm system works, I guess," she said, propped against him as he closed the door and pressed the button for the foyer, the bottom floor for that particular lift.

"What alarm system?"

"You know, the one Ryan had installed."

"I never heard the alarm, Des. Ryan and I both had a bad feeling when he couldn't reach you by phone." He grimaced. "Actually, it was as though someone was telling me to get to you. I had the strongest feeling something was wrong. I thought I was being stupid."

"You weren't." She rubbed the back of her neck. "It was probably my parents urging you to get to me."

"What?"

"Never mind. I'll explain later. I wish there was a phone with an outside line here. That one"—she pointed to the control panel—"calls security only. I don't trust any of the security guards right now. At least one of them works for Kimberley Marchese and Roger Curlew."

"They're the skunks in the woodpile?"

She nodded.

When the elevator stopped, they looked at each other.

"We have to move carefully," she whispered.

They both looked out the small window. No one was in sight.

"Should we try it?" Damian whispered. "Why

are we talking so low? No one could hear us in here."

"Open it." She assumed a defensive jujitsu stance. "Get ready."

The doors eased back. Slipping out first with Damian behind her, she eyed their surroundings.

"Looks clear," Damian muttered. "My car's on the side street. I came in that way."

"We're leaving the same way." As she turned she heard a flurry from the front of the lobby.

Suddenly an angry Brace burst through the entrance, Ryan right behind him. Brace glanced all around, then fixed on her. "Dammit, Destiny," he said as he raced across the space between them. He caught her up in arms.

"Darling, I'm fine. Damian saved me."

Still holding her, Brace looked at her friend. "I owe you, big time." Then he stiffened. "Saved you? From what?"

"I'll tell you later. Let's get out of here."

She again turned toward the side entrance when a voice behind them stopped her.

"What a nice little get-together," Kimberley Marchese said.

Brace whirled around, pushing Destiny behind him.

"She's part of the problem," Destiny muttered.

"Put the gun down, Marchese. The police are coming and—"

"I don't think so. You're bluffing, Coolidge,"

Roger Curlew said, crossing the lobby to stand next to Kimberley.

"He's not," Destiny said. "I pushed a button on my desk that summons the authorities."

"We'll see about that," Kimberley said, her jaw locked.

"Worry not, Kim. He'll handle it. He'll be there to meet anyone who tries to get in. We'll handle these particular problems." Roger's smile was nasty. "This is great. Finally we get them together. It's time to put an end to this, I think."

"Put an end to what?" Brace asked, his gaze roving the area.

"Don't try to stall. Your friend Webb isn't coming. He should've been more careful about his help." Roger grinned. "Ex-CIA and he only spot-checks the cleaning crew coming into his home. Foolish man. He's already been taken care of."

"I see," Brace said. How had Webb managed to be ambushed? It didn't fit what he knew of the man. "You'd better give this up, Curlew. You and Marchese have broken the law. You're going to jail on a number of counts. I don't think you want to risk the gas chamber."

"You know nothing," Curlew growled. He looked at Marchese. "Keep the gun trained on them. We're going with the plan."

Brace eyed Ryan, who gave an infinitesimal nod. He readied himself and was about to leap when two uniformed guards showed themselves.

"Where the hell you been?" Curlew barked.

"Someone knocked out Baker," one of them said. "We were looking for the intruder."

"We've got them all. Watch them."

Brace ground his teeth. They'd have to make a break at another time, but it would have to be soon. Curlew seemed anxious. The thing to do was try to talk to them. "Listen, you men, at this point you've only broken some—"

"You're repeating yourself," Curlew said.

"Wait!" another voice called. Brace looked around for its source.

"Uncle Tyrrell," Destiny whispered. "Be careful."

Roger laughed.

Destiny stiffened, then glanced at her uncle, her gaze narrowing.

"Beginning to suspect, my dear?" Tyrrell said.

"What are you saying?"

Tyrrell took a deep breath. "Something I've wanted to say for too long. It's over, Destiny. God knows I tried to do it neatly."

"The way you arranged a drive-by shooting for her mother," Brace said, "so that the authorities would call it random, instead of the well-planned murder it was. And the way you hired those thugs to take care of Destiny." His soft tone seemed to bounce off the floor tiles.

Tyrrell's face changed into a hard mask. "So, you figured it out."

"Yes. Actually Webb's investigation tied it together." He turned to Destiny. "I was waiting for a few final pieces of evidence to come in before I told you, Des."

Destiny stared at Tyrrell. "You killed my mother," she said from a throat gone dry as dust.

Tyrrell grimaced. "I had no plans to hurt anyone . . . even though I'd been overlooked far too long. I made this company what it is."

"You?" Brace scoffed. "Everyone knows that the construction machine patents that got this company started were Porter's and Mason's. *Their* ideas, *their* drive, built the business."

Tyrrell's face purpled. "They were idea men. I was the doer, the worker. I brought the right people to them. I put it together."

"Can we forget this?" Kimberley said. "What if the police are on the way?"

"They aren't. Besides, you've been paid well enough," Tyrrell snarled, silencing her. "It's about time someone knew what I've suffered."

"Suffered?" Brace repeated, goading the older man. "You make a million-dollar salary off a company started, funded, and nurtured by others. Where's the pain in that? You've lived off the Smiths since your high school days. You're owed nothing."

Destiny stared at Tyrrell. "Why did my mother have to die?"

"Lynn was nosy and smart. She accused me of skimming."

"Which you were," Brace said.

"I was taking what was rightfully mine," Tyrrell shouted.

Brace shook his head. "No, you were stealing from Porter and Mason. Lynn had you investigated."

Tyrrell's eyes bugged from his head. "That's not true."

"Sure it is, but you had her killed before she could find any definitive proof."

"They were fools! I was in love with Cordelia. Mason knew that, but he chased after her. She was mine. He and Porter took everything."

"My aunt loved her husband," Destiny said. "How will she feel when she discovers what you've done?"

"She won't," Tyrrell growled. He looked at his comrades, gesturing that they take them.

Damian dove at Kimberley. He caught her, but not before she fired.

Ryan and Brace went after the others.

Caught between desperation and rage, Destiny thrust herself through the air, catching her uncle in the chest with her feet. They both went down, but when he tried to scramble for the gun that Kimberley had dropped, Destiny chopped him across the jaw. He fell back. "You snake." She leaned over him, hands poised to finish him with two downward chops.

"Not only her," Tyrrell gasped, raising his hands to protect himself, hatred frothing from his mouth. "Your uncle and father too. The elevator accident was arranged by me. They deserved it."

Shocked, Destiny went flaccid.

Tyrrell, though heavier than he should be, moved

fast. He rolled, grabbing for the fallen gun. A wounded Damian tried to stop him. Kimberley, still dazed, struggled toward the weapon too. She reached it first and turned it on Destiny. Damian threw himself on her again, striking the weapon, deflecting the shot just as the gun fired.

"Des!" Brace shouted.

"I'm all right."

Then in a flurry of shouts and warning shots, the police arrived, with Webb and Hedges close behind.

Destiny, still dazed, sat back on the floor.

Brace threw himself down beside her, cuddling her close. "Tell me you're fine. Please."

"I am. No problems. She missed."

"No, she didn't," a panting Ryan said, holding Damian and his bloodied arm. "He fared worse." He jerked his chin toward Tyrrell.

"Oh," Destiny whispered. "Is he dead?"

Webb nodded. "Clean through the heart."

"It was an accident," Kimberley said, her voice strained.

Curlew glared at her, then at the dead Tyrrell.

Brace hugged Destiny and looked over at Curlew and Marchese. "I guess you won't get paid. All the deals Tyrrell made are canceled."

FIFTEEN

Destiny was sitting on the wide semicircular porch overlooking the lake, her three-month-old baby asleep in a carry-crib next to her. Ryan and Damian had taken Jeremy and Ella to the beach.

It was June, the sun was shining, the lake water warming in the long, hot days. Summer had come again to Yokapa County.

Brace exited the house, hunkering down next to her chair. He studied her for a moment. "Tears. Were you thinking about your parents again?"

"Yes." She leaned against him. "I'll never forget how they saved me."

"They loved you. They'll always be a presence in our life."

"Thank you," she said, a husky catch in her throat.

"We've had a wonderful second chance."

She nodded. "It's almost a year since I found the children and you showed up on my doorstep."

He kissed her again. "Yes." He stayed quiet, sensing she needed to talk.

"In some ways it seems like yesterday. Other times it's as though we've been a family for years."

"How do you think your parents would feel about our burgeoning family?"

She smiled. "They'd be delighted. My mother was only able to have one child." She sighed. "I suppose it's silly to be so certain they warned me, but I am."

"So am I."

"And now Curlew and Marchese are doing a long stretch in prison. It's justice." Her eyes shut for a moment. "It still seems unreal."

"I know it was hard to explain to Cordelia."

Destiny nodded. "Donald was wonderful. He wouldn't let her blame herself. I certainly didn't want that."

"She knows you love her, Des."

"I hope so."

"Believe it. That's why she visits with us so often. She wouldn't do that if she felt any resentment or guilt."

"I know."

When her husband kissed her, she twined her arms around his neck. "I love you, Brace. You've made me so happy."

He kissed her again. "I love you too. And I have something to show you." He frowned. "In some ways I suppose I shouldn't, but I want this cleared up once and for all." He placed a tattered notebook in her lap.

Puzzled, she opened it. When she saw Tyrrell's name, she almost shut it again. Then a notation caught her eye. She read for a few minutes, then looked at Brace. "These are Webb's case notes, proving your suspicions were correct. Tyrrell had you drugged and put you in those positions with that woman."

He nodded. "Webb even found the woman." His smile twisted. "Webb surmises that Tyrrell thought he would have more power over you if you and I were separated."

She shook her head. "None of us suspected how twisted he was." They were both silent for a minute, with Brace gently stroking her hair.

"You look wonderful," he finally said. He glanced at the sleeping baby. "So does our little boy."

She smiled. "Porter Smith Coolidge should've been named after you."

Brace shook his head. "No. Your father was a man among men. He didn't know how to be mean or small. That's the way I want our Porter to be."

"He'll be like you."

He grinned. "You're so damned quick. You have the best brain, the most beautiful body, the most courageous spirit of anyone in the world. Have I told you I adore you?"

"Not enough, never enough." She smiled at him, cocking her head. "I'm so confident and eager for life." Her smile faded. "What if I'd lost you through my stupidity?"

"Couldn't happen. I'd follow you anywhere and everywhere."

Relief was in her sigh. "Don't change."

"Not a chance."

A yelp at the top of the stairs leading up from the beach turned their heads.

"Des!" Damian yelled. "Your son is just like you. He dunked me."

Ryan laughed, sweeping Ella into his arms. "Ella and Jeremy won the water war."

Brace kissed his wife, then rose to his feet. "I suppose I should see to this." He leered down at her. "Tonight, beautiful lady, when we're alone, you can have your way with me."

"Count on it." She watched him leave the porch and join the noisy foursome on the deck overlooking the lake.

She started to laugh, then felt a coolness brush her skin. Turning her head, she looked right into her father's eyes. "I see you so clearly now."

"I'm glad. It's time for us to leave you, child, but we'll be with you always, even though you don't see us."

Her mother smiled. "Your family's wonderful. We had to tell you that."

"Thank you for what you did."

They nodded, then leaned forward to see the baby. They beamed.

"He's wonderful."

Destiny nodded at her mother, touched and bemused. "What do you think of Jeremy and Ella?"

"They're perfect, of course," her mother said.

Destiny chuckled. Then she was aware of them moving away. She could see them approach the quintet still arguing and laughing.

When there was a stillness among those on the deck, Destiny stiffened. Had they seen her parents?

After a moment, her parents vanished and the others started toward her. Brace, Ryan and Damian looked wary.

"The nice lady and man love us, Mama," Ella said. "They said so."

"Yeah," Jeremy said. "That's what they said to me too. They were nice." Jeremy threw himself into her arms. Ella followed suit. "Mrs. Duggan is making us cookies. May we have some?"

Destiny hugged them close and nodded, not able to speak.

THE EDITORS' CORNER

To celebrate our fifteenth anniversary, we have decided to couple this month with a very special theme. For many, the paranormal has always been intriguing, whether it's mystical convergences, the space-time continuum, the existence of aliens, or speculation about the afterlife. We went to our own LOVESWEPT authors and asked them to come up with their most intriguing ideas. And thus the EX-TRAORDINARY LOVERS theme month was born. Have fun with this taste of the supernatural, but first check beneath the bed, then snuggle under the covers. And don't let the bedbugs bite . . . they do exist, you know!

Brianne St. John is finding herself **NEVER ALONE,** in Cheryln Biggs's LOVESWEPT #890. It's hard enough when just one ghost is hanging around, but what does a girl do when four insistent ghosts are on her case? Ever since she was a little girl, she's had Athos, Porthos, Aramis, and yes, even D'Artagnan to scare all her boyfriends away. Now that gorgeous entrepreneur Mace Calder has set foot in Leimonte Castle, the four musketeers are in an uproar! Mace has noticed that the lady of the house tends to mutter to herself a great deal, but for now he has other important matters to take care of. As Mace and Brianne draw closer, strange things keep happening, objects are being moved, shadows are darkening doorways—and Mace wonders just when is that wall going to answer Brianne? Cheryln Biggs revisits old haunts and legends in this enchanting romp of a love story!

Journalist Nate Wagner has his hands full when he confronts **WITCHY WOMAN** Tess DeWitt, in LOVESWEPT #891 by Karen Leabo. What strikes Nate about the beautiful woman he's followed into a Back Bay antique shop is that she doesn't look like the notorious Moonbeam Majick, a witch who disappeared fifteen years ago. Tess knew she and everyone around her were in harm's way the minute she came across the cursed cat statue that had very nearly ruined her life. Teamed up with an insatiably curious Nate, Tess must find a way to save her best friend's life, prevent Nate from dying, and keep the cat away from the mysterious stranger who's bent on unleashing the statue's unholy powers. In the end, will a spell cast from loving hearts be enough to save them all from certain death? Karen Leabo delves into the mystical connections our souls offer to those we truly love.

Loveswept veteran Peggy Webb gives us **NIGHT OF THE DRAGON**, LOVESWEPT #892. With only a book and an ancient ring to guide her, Lydia

Star falls back in time and lands at the feet of a fire-breathing dragon. Lydia is saved by one of King Arthur's brave knights, Sir Dragon, and is forced to face the fact that she's not in San Diego anymore. Dragon is bewildered by his mysterious prisoner, but can't help being captivated by her ethereal beauty. Convinced that she is the result of some deviltry, he confides in the king's counsel, Merlyn. Lydia knows her time is running out and longs for the comforts of home, a fact that keeps her trying desperately to escape from the overbearing knight's clutches. Can this warrior be the keeper of her soul? Better yet, will he survive the journey to his heart's true home? Peggy Webb more than answers these questions with this sensual dream of a romance.

Catherine Mulvany treats us to **AQUAMARINE**, LOVESWEPT #893. Teague Harris can't believe his eyes when he sees his supposedly dead fiancée walking around the carnival grounds. He's even more surprised when he realizes that Shea McKenzie might not be his former love . . . but she does look enough like Kirsten Rainey to pose as the missing heiress for Kirsten's dying father. Drawn to Idaho by a postcard found among her dead mother's things, Shea reluctantly agrees to the outrageous masquerade after seeing a picture of a man who could pass for her own father. Then, as Shea discovers a cluster of glowing aquamarine crystals, she begins to experience Kirsten's memories. Can Shea trust Teague, a man who seems more interested in trying to solve the murder of Shea's twin than in moving on with the rest of his life? Catherine Mulvany teaches us that love is the strongest force on earth!

Happy reading!

With warmest wishes,

Susann Brailey   *Joy Abella*

Susann Brailey   Joy Abella
Senior Editor   Administrative Editor

P.S. Look for these women's fiction titles coming in June! From Nora Roberts comes **GENUINE LIES**, now in hardcover for the first time ever. Hollywood legend Eve Benedict selects Julia Summers to write her biography. Sparks fly and danger looms as three Hollywood players attempt to protect what they value most. Talented author Jane Feather introduces an irresistible new trilogy, beginning with **THE HOSTAGE BRIDE.** Three girls make a pact never to get married, but when Portia is accidentally kidnapped by a gang of outlaws, her hijacker gets more than he bargained for in his defiant and surprisingly attractive captive. And finally, Rebecca Kelley presents her debut, **THE WEDDING CHASE.** Zel Fleetwood is looking for a wealthy husband who can save her family. Instead she attracts the unwanted attentions of the earl of Northcliffe, whose ardent but misguided interest ruins her prospects. That is, until he realizes *he*'s the perfect match for her. And immediately following this page, preview the Bantam women's fiction titles on sale in May!

For current information on Bantam's women's fiction, visit our Web site at the following address:
http://www.bdd.com/romance

Don't miss these extraordinary
novels from Bantam Books!

On sale in May:

*A PLACE TO
CALL HOME*
by Deborah Smith

*THE WITCH AND
THE WARRIOR*
by Karyn Monk

Come home to the best-loved novel
of the year . . .

A Place to Call Home
BY *DEBORAH SMITH*

*Twenty years ago, Claire Maloney was the willful, pampered,
tomboyish daughter of the town's most respected family, but
that didn't stop her from befriending Roan Sullivan, a fierce,
motherless boy who lived in a rusted-out trailer amid junked
cars. No one in Dunderry, Georgia—least of all Claire's family—could understand the bond between these two mavericks.
But Roan and Claire belonged together . . . until the dark
afternoon when violence and terror overtook them, and Roan
disappeared from Claire's life. Now, two decades later, Claire
is adrift, and the Maloneys are still hoping the past can be
buried under the rich Southern soil. But Roan Sullivan is
about to walk back into their lives. . . . By turns tender and
sexy and heartbreaking and exuberant, A Place to Call
Home is an enthralling journey between two hearts—and a
deliciously original novel from one of the most imaginative
and appealing new voices in Southern fiction.*

"A beautiful, believable love story."
—*Chicago Tribune*

It started the year I performed as a tap-dancing leprechaun at the St. Patrick's Day carnival and Roanie Sullivan threatened to cut my cousin Carlton's throat with a
rusty pocketknife. That was also the year the Beatles
broke up and the National Guard killed four students at

Kent State, and Josh, who was in Vietnam, wrote home to Brady, who was a senior at Dunderry High, *Don't even think about enlisting. There's nothing patriotic about this shit.*

But I was only five years old; my world was narrow, deep, self-satisfied, well-off, very Southern, securely bound to the land and to a huge family descended almost entirely from Irish immigrants who had settled in the Georgia mountains over one hundred and thirty years ago. As far as I was concerned, life revolved in simple circles with me at the center.

The St. Patrick's Day carnival was nothing like it is now. There were no tents set up to dispense green beer, no artists selling handmade 24-karat-gold shamrock jewelry, no Luck of the Irish 5K Road Race, no imported musicians playing authentic Irish jigs on the town square. Now it's a *festival*, one of the top tourist events in the state.

But when I was five it was just a carnival, held in the old Methodist campground arbor east of town. The Jaycees and the Dunderry Ladies' Association sold barbecue sandwiches, green sugar cookes, and lime punch at folding tables in a corner next to the arbor's wooden stage, the Down Mountain Boys played bluegrass music, and the beginners' tap class from my Aunt Gloria's School of Dance was decked out in leprechaun costumes and forced into a mid-year minirecital.

Mama took snapshots of me in my involuntary servitude. I was not a born dancer. I had no rhythm, I was always out of step, and I disliked mastering anyone's routines but my own. I stood there on the stage, staring resolutely at the camera in my green-checkered bibbed dress with its ruffled skirt and a puffy white blouse, my green socks and black patent-leather tap shoes with green bows, my hair parted in fat red braids tied with green ribbons.

I looked like an unhappy Irish Heidi.

My class, all twenty of us, stomped and shuffled through our last number, accompanied by a tune from some Irish dance record I don't remember, which Aunt Gloria played full blast on her portable stereo connected to the Down Mountain Boys' big amplifiers. I looked down and there he was, standing in the crowd at the lip of the stage, a tall, shabby, ten-year-old boy with greasy black hair. Roan Sullivan. *Roanie.* Even in a small town the levels of society are a steep staircase. My family was at the top. Roan and his daddy weren't just at the bottom; they were in the cellar.

He watched me seriously, as if I weren't making a fool of myself, which I was. I had already accidentally stomped on my cousin Violet's left foot twice, and I'd elbowed my cousin Rebecca in her right arm, so they'd given me a wide berth on either side.

I forgot about my humiliating arms and feet and concentrated on Roanie Sullivan avidly, because it was the first close look I'd gotten at nasty, no-account Big Roan Sullivan's son from Sullivan's Hollow. We didn't associate with Big Roan Sullivan, even though he and Roanie were our closest neighbors on Soap Falls Road. The Hollow might as well have been on the far side of China, not two miles from our farm.

"That godforsaken hole only produces one thing— *trash.*" That's what Uncle Pete and Uncle Bert always said about the Hollow. And because everybody knew Roanie Sullivan was trash—came from it, looked like it, and smelled like it—they steered clear of him in the crowd. Maybe that was one reason I couldn't take my eyes off him. We were both human islands stuck in the middle of a lonely, embarrassing sea of space.

My cousin Carlton lounged a couple of feet away, between Roanie and the Jaycees' table. There are some relatives you just tolerate, and Carlton Maloney was in that group. He was about twelve, smug and well-fed, and he was laughing at me so hard that his eyes nearly disappeared in his face. He and my brother Hop were in the seventh grade together. Hop said he cheated on math tests. He was a weasel.

I saw him glance behind him. Once, twice. Uncle Dwayne was in charge of the Jaycees' food table and Aunt Rhonda was talking to him about something, so he was looking at her dutifully. He'd left a couple of dollar bills beside the cardboard shoe box he was using as a cash till.

Carlton eased one hand over, snatched the money, and stuck it in his trouser pocket.

I was stunned. He'd stolen from the Jaycees. He'd stolen from his own *uncle*. My brothers and I had been trained to such a strict code of honor that we wouldn't pilfer so much as a penny from the change cup on Daddy's dresser. I admit I had a weakness for the bags of chocolate chips in the bakery section of the grocery store, and if one just *happened* to fall off the shelf and burst open, I'd sample a few. But nonedible property was sacred. And stealing *money* was unthinkable.

Uncle Dwayne looked down at the table. He frowned. He hunted among packages of sugar cookies wrapped in cellophane and tied with green ribbons. He leaned toward Carlton and said something to him. From the stage I couldn't hear what he said—I couldn't hear anything except the music pounding in my ears—but I saw Carlton draw back dramatically, shaking his head. Then he turned and pointed at Roanie.

I was struck tapless. I simply couldn't move a foot. I stood there, rooted in place, and was dimly, painfully aware of people laughing at me, of my grandparents hiding their smiles behind their hands, and of Mama's and

Daddy's bewildered stares. Daddy, who could not dance either, waved his big hands helpfully, as if I was a scared calf he could shoo into moving again.

But I wasn't scared. I was furious.

Uncle Dwayne, his jaw thrust out, pushed his way around the table and grabbed Roanie by one arm. I saw Uncle Dwayne speak forcefully to him. I saw the blank expression on Roanie's face turn to sullen anger. I guess it wasn't the first time he'd been accused of something he didn't do.

His eyes darted to Carlton. He lunged at him. They went down in a heap, with Carlton on the bottom. People scattered, yelling. The whole Leprechaun Review came to a wobbly halt. Aunt Gloria bounded to her portable record player and the music ended with a screech like an amplified zipper. I bolted down the stairs at that end of the stage and squirmed through the crowd of adults.

Uncle Dwayne was trying to pull Roanie off Carlton, but Roanie had one hand wound in the collar of Carlton's sweater. He had the other at Carlton's throat, with the point of a rusty little penknife poised beneath Carlton's Adam's apple. "I didn't take no money!" Roanie yelled at him. "You damn liar!"

Daddy plowed into the action. He planted a knee in Roanie's back and wrenched the knife out of his hand. He and Uncle Dwayne pried the boys apart, and Daddy pulled Roanie to his feet. "He has a knife," I heard someone whisper. "That Sullivan boy's vicious."

"Where's that money?" Uncle Dwayne thundered, peering down into Roanie Sullivan's face. "Give it to me. Right now."

"I ain't got no money. I didn't take no money." He mouthed words like a hillbilly, kind of honking them out half finished. He had a crooked front tooth with jagged edges, too. It flashed like a lopsided fang.

"Oh, yeah, you did," Carlton yelled. "I saw you! Everybody knows you steal stuff! Just like your daddy!"

"Roanie, hand over the money," Daddy said. Daddy had a booming voice. He was fair, but he was tough. "Don't make me go through your pockets," he added sternly. "Come on, boy, tell the truth and give the money back."

"I ain't *got* it."

I was plastered to the sidelines but close enough to see the misery and defensiveness in Roanie's face. Oh, lord. He was the kind of boy who fought and cussed and put a knife to people's throats. He caused trouble. He deserved trouble.

But he's not a thief.

Don't tattle on Carlton. Maloneys stick together. We're big, that way.

But it's not fair.

"All right, Roanie," Daddy said, and reached for the back pocket of Roanie's dirty jeans.

"He didn't take it," I said loudly. "Carlton did!" Everyone stared at me. Well, I'd gotten used to that. I met Roanie Sullivan's wary, surprised eyes. He could burn a hole through me with those eyes.

Uncle Dwayne glared at me. "Now, Claire. Are you sure you're not getting back at Carlton because he spit boiled peanuts at you outside Sunday school last week?"

No, but I knew how a boiled peanut felt. Hot, real hot. "Roanie didn't take the money," I repeated. I jabbed a finger at Carlton. "Carlton did. I *saw* him, Daddy. I saw him stick it in his front pocket."

Daddy and Uncle Dwayne pivoted slowly. Carlton's face, already sweaty and red, turned crimson. "*Carlton,*" Uncle Dwayne said.

"She's just picking on me!"

Uncle Dwayne stuck a hand in Carlton's pocket and pulled out two wadded-up dollar bills.

And that was that.

Uncle Dwayne hauled Carlton off to find Uncle Eugene and Aunt Arnetta, Carlton's folks. Daddy let go of Roanie Sullivan. "Go on. Get out of here."

"He pulled that knife, Holt," Uncle Pete said behind me.

Daddy scowled. "He couldn't cut his way out of a paper sack with a knife that little."

"But he *pulled* it on Carlton."

"Forget about it, Pete. Go on, everybody."

Roanie stared at me. I held his gaze as if hypnotized. Isolation radiated from him like an invisible shield, but there was this *gleam* in his eyes, made up of surprise and gratitude and suspicion, bearing on me like concentrated fire, and I felt singed. Daddy put a hand on the collar of the faded, floppy football jersey he wore and dragged him away. I started to follow, but Mama had gotten through the crowd by then, and she snagged me by the back of my dress. "Hold on, Claire Karleen Maloney. You've put on enough of a show."

Dazed, I looked up at her. Hop and Evan peered at me from her side. Violet and Rebecca watched me, open-mouthed. A whole bunch of Maloneys scrutinized me. "Carlton's a weasel," I explained finally.

Mama nodded. "You told the truth. That's fine. You're done. I'm proud of you."

"Then how come everybody's lookin' at me like I'm weird?"

"Because you *are*," Rebecca blurted out. "Aren't you scared of Roanie Sullivan?"

"He didn't laugh at me when I was dancing. I think he's okay."

"You've got a strange way of sortin' things out," Evan said.

"She's one brick short of a load," Hop added.

So that was the year I realized Roanie was not just trashy, not just different, he was dangerous, and taking his side was a surefire way to seed my own mild reputation as a troublemaker and Independent Thinker.

I was fascinated by him from then on.

"An enthralling tale of two compelling, heartwarming characters and the healing power of love . . . I loved it!"—Elizabeth Thornton, author of *You Only Love Twice*

The historical tales of Karyn Monk are filled with unforgettable romance and her own special brand of warmth and humor. Now love casts its spell in the Highlands, as a warrior seeks a miracle from a mysterious lady of secrets and magic. . . .

The Witch and the Warrior
BY KARYN MONK

Suspected of witchcraft, Gwendolyn MacSween has been condemned to being burned at the stake at the hands of her own clan. Yet rescue comes from a most unlikely source. Mad Alex MacDunn, laird of the mighty rival clan MacDunn, is a man whose past is scarred with tragedy and loss. His last hope lies in capturing the witch of the MacSweens—and using her magic to heal his dying son. He expects to find an old hag. . . . Instead he finds a young woman of unearthly beauty. There's only one problem: Gwendolyn has no power to bewitch or to heal. Now she must pretend to be a sorceress—or herself perish. But can she use her common sense to save Alex's son, and her natural powers as a woman to enchant a fierce and handsome Highland warrior—before a dangerous enemy destroys them both?

Gwendolyn regarded the sky in bewilderment. She had never witnessed such an abrupt change in the weather.

"Everything is fine," she assured them loudly. "The spirits have heard my plea."

They remained in their circle, watching the sky as a cool gale whipped their hair and clothes. And then, just as suddenly as it burst upon them, the storm died. The wind gasped and was gone, and the clouds melted into the darkness, unveiling the silent, tranquil glow of the moon and stars once again.

"By God, that was something!" roared Cameron, slapping Brodick heartily on the back. "Have you ever seen such a thing?"

"Did you see that, Alex?" demanded Brodick, looking uneasy.

"Aye," said Alex. "I saw."

Brodick raised his arm and cautiously flexed it at the elbow. "I think my arm feels better." He sounded more troubled than pleased.

"I *know* my head feels better!" said Cameron happily. "What about you, Neddie?"

"I have no wounds for the witch to heal," said Ned, shrugging. He frowned, then shrugged again. "That's odd," he remarked, slowly turning his head from side to side. "My neck has been stiff and aching for a week, and suddenly it feels fine."

Gwendolyn folded her arms across her chest and regarded them triumphantly. Clearly just the suggestion that they would feel better had had an effect on them, which was what she had hoped would happen. Luckily, the weather had complemented her little performance.

"Can you cast that spell on anyone?" asked Cameron, still excited.

"Not everyone," she replied carefully. "And my spells don't always work."

"What do you mean?" demanded Alex.

"The success of a spell depends on many things," she replied evasively. She did not want him to think she could simply say a few words and fell an entire army. "My powers will not work on everyone."

"I don't give a damn if they work on everyone," he growled. "As long as they work on one person." His expression was harsh. "Cameron, take the first watch. The rest of you get some sleep. We ride at first light."

Brodick produced an extra plaid from his horse and carefully draped it over Isabella's unconscious form. Then he lay down just a few feet away from her, where he could watch over her during the night. Ned and MacDunn also stretched out upon the ground, arranging part of their plaids over their shoulders for warmth.

"Do you sleep standing up?" MacDunn asked irritably.

"No," replied Gwendolyn.

"Then lie down," he orderd. "We still have a long journey ahead."

She had assumed they were going to bind her to a tree. But with Cameron watching her, she would not get very far if she attempted to escape tonight. Obviously that was what MacDunn believed. Relieved that she would not be tied, she wearily lowered herself to the ground.

Tomorrow would be soon enough to find an opportunity for escape.

The little camp grew quiet, except for the occasional snap of the fire. Soon the rumble of snoring began to drift lazily through the air. Gwendolyn wondered how they had all managed to find sleep so quickly in such uncomfortable conditions. The fire had died and the ground was damp and cold, forcing her to curl into a tight ball and wrap her bare arms around herself. It didn't help. With every passing moment her flesh grew more chilled, until finally her entire body was shivering uncontrollably.

"Gwendolyn," called MacDunn in a low voice, "come here."

She sat up and peered at him through the darkness. "Why?" she demanded suspiciously.

"Because your chattering teeth are keeping me awake," he grumbled. "You will lie next to me and share my plaid."

She stared at him in horror. "I am fine, MacDunn," she hastily assured him. "You needn't concern yourself about—"

"Come here," he repeated firmly.

"No," she replied, shaking her head. "I may be your prisoner, but I will *not* share your bed."

She waited for him to argue. Instead he muttered something under his breath, adjusted his plaid more to his liking over his naked chest and closed his eyes once again. Satisfied that she had won this small but critical battle, she vigorously rubbed her arms to warm them, then primly curled onto the ground.

Her teeth began to chatter so violently she had to bite down hard to try to control them.

The next thing she knew, MacDunn was stretching out beside her and wrapping his plaid over both of them.

"Don't you dare touch me!" Gwendolyn hissed, rolling away.

MacDunn grabbed her waist and firmly drew her back, imprisoning her in the warm crook of his enormous, barely clad body.

"Be still!" he ordered impatiently.

"I will not be still, you foul, mad ravisher of women!" She kicked him as hard as she could in his shin.

"Jesus—" he swore, loosening his hold slightly.

Gwendolyn tried to scramble away from him, but he instantly tightened his grip.

"Listen to me!" he commanded, somehow managing to keep his voice low. "I have no intention of bedding you, do you understand?"

Gwendolyn glared at him, her breasts rising and falling so rapidly they grazed his bandaged chest.

"I may be considered mad," he continued, "but to my knowledge I have not yet earned a reputation as a ravager of unwilling women—do you understand?"

His blue eyes held hers. She tried to detect deceit in them, but could not. All she saw was anger, mingled with weariness.

"I have already risked far more than I have a right to, to save your life and take you home with me, Gwendolyn MacSween," he continued. "I will *not* have it end by watching you fall deathly ill from the chill of the night."

He waited a moment, allowing his comments to penetrate her fear. Then, cautiously, he loosened his grip. "Lie still," he ordered gruffly. "I will keep you warm, nothing more. You have my word."

She regarded him warily. "You swear you will not abuse me, MacDunn? On your honor?"

"I swear."

Reluctantly, she eased herself onto her side. MacDunn adjusted part of his plaid over her, then once again fitted himself around her. His arm circled her waist, drawing her into the warm, hard cradle of his body. Gwendolyn lay there rigidly for a long while, scarcely breathing, waiting for him to break his word.

Instead, he began to snore.

Heat seemed to radiate from him, slowly permeating

her chilled flesh. It warmed even the soft wool of his plaid, she realized, snuggling further into it. A deliciously masculine scent wafted around her, the scent of horse and leather and woods. Little by little, the feel of MacDunn's powerful body against hers became more comforting than threatening, especially as his snores grew louder.

Until that moment, she had had virtually no knowledge of physical contact. Her mother had died when she was very young, and her father, though loving, had never been at ease with open demonstrations of affection. The unfamiliar sensation of MacDunn's warm body wrapped protectively around her was unlike anything she had ever imagined. She was his prisoner. And yet, she felt impossibly safe.

"You belong to me now," he had told her. *"I protect what is mine."* She belonged to no one. She reflected drowsily, and no one could protect her from men like Robert, or the ignorance and fear that was sure to fester in MacDunn's own clan the moment they saw her. She would escape him long before they reached his lands. Tomorrow, she would break free from these warriors, so she could retrieve the stone, return to her clan and kill Robert. Above all else, Robert must die. She would make him pay for murdering her father and destroying her life.

But all this seemed distant and shadowy as she drifted into slumber, sheltered by this brave, mad warrior, whose heart pulsed steadily against her back.

On sale in June:

GENUINE LIES
by Nora Roberts

THE HOSTAGE BRIDE
by Jane Feather

THE WEDDING CHASE
by Rebecca Kelley

Bestselling Historical Women's Fiction

❧ AMANDA QUICK ❧

____28354-5 SEDUCTION ...$6.50/$8.99 Canada

____28932-2 SCANDAL ....$6.50/$8.99

____28594-7 SURRENDER ....$6.50/$8.99

____29325-7 RENDEZVOUS ....$6.50/$8.99

____29315-X RECKLESS ....$6.50/$8.99

____29316-8 RAVISHED ....$6.50/$8.99

____29317-6 DANGEROUS ....$6.50/$8.99

____56506-0 DECEPTION ....$6.50/$8.99

____56153-7 DESIRE ....$6.50/$8.99

____56940-6 MISTRESS ....$6.50/$8.99

____57159-1 MYSTIQUE ....$6.50/$7.99

____57190-7 MISCHIEF ....$6.50/$8.99

____57407-8 AFFAIR ....$6.99/$8.99

❧ IRIS JOHANSEN ❧

____29871-2 LAST BRIDGE HOME ...$5.50/$7.50

____29604-3 THE GOLDEN

BARBARIAN ....$6.99/$8.99

____29244-7 REAP THE WIND .....$5.99/$7.50

____29032-0 STORM WINDS ....$6.99/$8.99

Ask for these books at your local bookstore or use this page to order.

Please send me the books I have checked above. I am enclosing $____ (add $2.50 to cover postage and handling). Send check or money order, no cash or C.O.D.'s, please.

Name _____

Address _____

City/State/Zip _____

Send order to: Bantam Books, Dept. FN 16, 2451 S. Wolf Rd., Des Plaines, IL 60018
Allow four to six weeks for delivery.

Prices and availability subject to change without notice.   FN 16 3/98

Bestselling Historical Women's Fiction

⚥ IRIS JOHANSEN ⚥

____28855-5 THE WIND DANCER . . .$5.99/$6.99

____29968-9 THE TIGER PRINCE . . .$6.99/$8.99

____29944-1 THE MAGNIFICENT
ROGUE . . . .$6.99/$8.99

____29945-X BELOVED SCOUNDREL .$6.99/$8.99

____29946-8 MIDNIGHT WARRIOR . .$6.99/$8.99

____29947-6 DARK RIDER . . . .$6.99/$8.99

____56990-2 LION'S BRIDE . . . .$6.99/$8.99

____56991-0 THE UGLY DUCKLING. . .$5.99/$7.99

____57181-8 LONG AFTER MIDNIGHT.$6.99/$8.99

____10616-3 AND THEN YOU DIE.... $22.95/$29.95

⚥ TERESA MEDEIROS ⚥

____29407-5 HEATHER AND VELVET .$5.99/$7.50

____29409-1 ONCE AN ANGEL . . . . .$5.99/$7.99

____29408-3 A WHISPER OF ROSES .$5.99/$7.99

____56332-7 THIEF OF HEARTS . . . . .$5.50/$6.99

____56333-5 FAIREST OF THEM ALL .$5.99/$7.50

____56334-3 BREATH OF MAGIC . . . .$5.99/$7.99

____57623-2 SHADOWS AND LACE . . .$5.99/$7.99

____57500-7 TOUCH OF
ENCHANTMENT. . . . .$5.99/$7.99

Ask for these books at your local bookstore or use this page to order.

Please send me the books I have checked above. I am enclosing $____ (add $2.50 to cover postage and handling). Send check or money order, no cash or C.O.D.'s, please.

Name _____

Address _____

City/State/Zip _____

Send order to: Bantam Books, Dept. FN 16, 2451 S. Wolf Rd., Des Plaines, IL 60018
Allow four to six weeks for delivery.
Prices and availability subject to change without notice.

FN 16 3/98